Legends
from Invalid Street

Legends
from Invalid Street
by
Efraim Sevela

Translated
by Anthony Kahn

1974
DOUBLEDAY & COMPANY, INC., GARDEN CITY, NEW YORK

ISBN: 0-385-01692-1
LIBRARY OF CONGRESS CATALOG CARD NUMBER 73-81448

To Marcel Laska,
my brother in France

ACKNOWLEDGMENT

I would like to express my deep thanks to Rita Brackman for her invaluable help in the final stages of this translation; to Boris E. Ross, for his assistance on 'A Different Story, Legend Number Five'; and to Jayne Chamberlin for the example of her keen wit and judgment at all times.

Tony Kahn

Contents

Contents

The
Road to Happiness

From the Author

There are lots of barbershops in Vilno, but none of them have names. Just numbers. Number One, Number Two, and so on. In the whole town only one shop had a name. It had a number too, of course, and you'd never find the name up on the sign. All the same, it existed, as they say, on people's lips. Literally everybody who found himself in Vilno around that time, Russian and Jew, Lithuanian and Pole, called that barbershop "The Road to Happiness." Only they'd say it in Polish, *Droga do Szczęs'-cia*, each in his own accent.

Why? I'll tell you.

Leading up to the entrance of that tiny shop, sheltered on the main floor of a large old home, right at the corner of Gedimin and Tatarsky streets, there were three steps. Out of real white marble. Where from nobody knew. A mystery. Maybe two hundred years before some Radziwill, or Count Pototsky at least, had ordered them for a palace. Anyway, here they were and people had to climb them to get to Barbershop Number—Number I—don't-know-what—to The Road to Happiness.

So where did the words come from? You'll want to know, of course, and I'll tell you. I don't know.

On each of the white marble steps a Polish word had been trimmed in red granite. On the bottom one *Droga*, on the middle *do*, and *Szczęs'cia* on the third. *Road—to—Happiness*. Now, does it make sense?

Picture this. A person on his way to a barbershop for a shave or a haircut. Maybe just a splash of cologne, who knows? Does happiness have anything to do with it? A silly idea. Still, what's his trip, all three steps of it? The Road to Happiness, no less.

If you were never there I feel sorry for you, that's all. Not because you lost your crack at happiness. You know what they say: Happiness doesn't depend on us much, and even less on a barbershop. Just because they shaved you and cut your hair doesn't mean they went and made all your dreams come true. Especially if you have to pay for it like anyplace else and not fixed rates either, but, as Yasha, the barber, puts it, "Whatever won't kill you."

I'm only saying that if you were never there you missed a lot. You want to know what I found there? All the stories I'm going to tell you under the title of *The Road to Happiness*. That's what.

Let's take it, as they say, from the top. First, I'll explain when it all happened. Where, you know already.

I don't live in Vilno myself. I just went back and forth a number of times and spent quite a while in the hotels. I was traveling on private business. The fact is I knew of a fur factory in Vilno where you could get a fair price on skins without too much trouble. The kind they make ladies' coats out of.

My wife wanted one, you see.

That's all, you ask? Nothing else?

I'll tell you. This time that was all.

So what kind of a husband would I be if I couldn't get my wife a little trifle like that? There was nothing to argue about. I climbed aboard a train and went to Vilno.

Jews are pretty much in charge of the fur manufacturing business. Everybody knows that. It's sort of a national profession with us, you might say. Just as with the Russians these days it's getting all the top jobs.

Supposedly there was a lot of money in being a furrier. Otherwise, why would Jews bother with it? Once, they say, at an autopsy they found so much fur down the lungs of a furrier you could have made a lady's jacket out of it and a hat besides. That's the story, anyway. The police even wanted to draw up a report charging embezzlement of Socialist property.

But that's beside the point. The fact is, buying those furs in Vilno turned out to be a lot harder than I thought. The Jews were afraid of thieving like the fire. The time for that kind of enterprise couldn't have been worse. I don't even like remembering what was going on. Jews, Jews, Jews, that's all the papers talked about. They'd brand everyone they could get their hands on as the vilest kind of foe—an agent of JOINT* or a British and American spy. In the streets they'd spit right in your face, for no reason at all. Even among us, in the arts, there were some who had me tagged as a Japanese spy. I got myself out of that one by agreeing to go far away on tour. Free of charge, too, as a "duty to society," to use the current phrase.

All in all, a great time to be alive. 1953. Right before Stalin died, when he'd lost his mind already and was permitting all kinds of violations of Socialist legality. That's what Khrushchev told us later. Not that Khrushchev was that crazy about us either. But that was his business. Nobody said you had to love us, just let us live.

You know what he'd have said if you'd told him that?

"What do you want, a cherry on top?"

He really liked folk sayings.

To get to the point: I didn't buy any furs, but I did waste a lot

* Branch of the United Jewish Appeal.

of cash. A real Jewish deal, as they say. So crafty, these Jews, you wouldn't believe it. Always on top. That time I was so much on top I barely scraped up enough for the ride back home.

Not that I regret what I lost. The pleasure I'd get visiting The Road to Happiness barbershop Sundays in Vilno you couldn't buy at any price. And now, if I manage to share it all with you, or even just a part, you'll be getting it for nothing and the pleasure will be double.

You're going to laugh at some of this, of course. So go ahead and laugh, it's good for you. But such a reason for laughter as the stories I'm going to tell, I'd wish only on our enemies. Maybe then they'd know what grief is all about.

Personally I've got nothing against laughter. I don't completely agree with Comrade Nichiporenko, the former master sergeant of my platoon. A clever man this was, even though he had trouble recalling what he'd read. He remembered the classic phrase "He who laughs last laughs best" only in the abridged version. "He who's last laughs," he'd teach us. And for our three years in the service of the Soviet Army we didn't laugh once. Not at least while the master sergeant was around.

And so to the point. No more side steps, no more running at the mouth. Otherwise, just stop me and tell me straight I'm off the track. All right?

So. When this was you know already. 1953. In case you've forgotten what good times we're living in now, one look at *Soviet Lithuania* would freshen your mind. Every day they'd post the latest issue of that newspaper on a wooden stand nailed to the wall of the barbershop to the left of the entrance. And every issue all they'd ever talk about was Jews. To listen to them you'd think that Soviet power didn't have another headache in the world. Their viewpoint, you can imagine, wasn't too friendly. Not to mention the caricatures with long, bent

Jewish noses they'd draw every day, as like each other as two peas in a pod. Assassins in lab coats they looked like, clutching poison in one hand and dollar bills in the other. Doctor Poisoners in a word.* Long, hook-nosed people without a friend or family tie. Actually the artist was pretty observant: the noses *were* good likenesses. He could even have drawn them straight from life, it seemed to me, right here by the barbershop.

Beneath the *Soviet Lithuania* newsstand, you see, there was a shoeshiner with his box and brushes. Chloineh, they called him, and he had a nose on him just like the one in the caricature over his head. That, however, was where the similarity ended.

Dollar bills and poison Chloineh didn't have. If he'd had the bills he wouldn't have been spending every winter and summer out in the open dressed in rags shining everybody else's shoes. And if he'd had the poison, he'd have used it long ago on himself. To end his suffering.

Besides, Chloineh had been awarded the Order of the Patriotic War, First Class. He'd fastened it to the lapel of his one and only jacket and there it stayed, no matter how smeared with black and yellow shoe cream it got. As it was, the silver and gilding of the decoration were already sunk beneath a layer of polish. Just to show he'd earned the order honestly at the Front and not bought it, his entire right leg was missing. Ripped off at the roots, as they say. Not even a stump left. That explains the smooth spot he'd sit on after stretching out his left leg on the sidewalk.

Chloineh was small, messy, and rumpled as a sparrow. The face around that classic nose was covered with a prickly, week-old growth of gray-black stubble, and his head was sunk in tousles that shot out from under his old service cap.

* This was the time of the notorious "Doctors' Plot," a supposed assassination scheme against Stalin involving prominent Jewish physicians.

On top of everything else Chloineh suffered from shell shock. When he'd speak he'd stutter, little bubbles of foam frothing on his chapped lips. To make matters worse he never shut up, except when his customer left him with a shine on his shoes and polish all up and down his pants.

Chloineh would engage every customer in a conversation. Actually he'd stare you in the knee and do all the talking himself, without even bothering to look up and see if you approved or not. Then he'd get so excited the foam would start bubbling at the corners of his lips and his brushes would scratch away at your boots, your socks, even your pants legs. So, Chloineh didn't have a regular clientele. One time with him and you'd have to take your pants or socks to the dry cleaners to get the spots of shoe polish off.

Chloineh got by on chance customers, novices who didn't know his style and would drop into his mess for the first and the last time.

I had Chloineh do my boots, too. Once. I wanted to give a Jew, an unhappy, one-legged war casualty, a chance to make some money. When he smeared my pants in one shot right up to the knee I didn't even call him names. I'd been under the spell of his monologue, an angry seizure of a speech that seemed completely out of place with that caricature hanging over his head. Just listen to what filled the head of a shell-shocked Jew in that happiest of times, 1953, right before Stalin died.

"A newcomer, eh? I can spot 'em right off!" Chloineh got right down to my boots and his monologue without even looking me in the face.

"I'm going to let you in on the whole story, too. A bunch of cheats, that's what they are, the whole lot of them, swindlers and cheats!"

He described a circle in the air with his brush that included everyone in earshot and all the rest of Vilno.

"You tell *me*. Is there any truth on earth or not?" The foam started bubbling in the corners of his lips.

I didn't know how to answer the question so I said nothing. They'd done him a great wrong, I was guessing, and now he was going to start complaining about the way his life had gone. Chloineh wasn't even waiting for my answer.

"Swindlers, that's all, and as for the truth, forget it! You know who they just made rabbi in Kovno?" Chloineh choked with indignation and the brush with the polish reached my knee. "I know who! We were in the Sixteenth Division together. In Balakhna, when we were getting into units, we slept on bunks side by side. The way he guzzled pork! Not just from the head either, but the rear, the rear! Now you understand who they made rabbi in Kovno? So, I ask you, is there truth on earth?"

I tried my best to calm him down, if only to save my poor pants. There wasn't any reason to get upset, I said, now was the time for Jews to be thinking about other things like pulling through these hard times. Most of all, I told him, don't get so nervous.

Chloineh came back at me with such a devastating argument, it left me speechless. Knocked my reasons inside out, that's how stunning his logic was.

"I've got a right to be nervous," he said, with a fire in his eyes like a madman, "when my thing is longer than my leg!"

I paid him more than I had to and left without a word. In badly polished boots. And spots of polish up and down my pants.

Off to the barbershop. To The Road to Happiness.

It was Sunday, a day of rest. The barbershop was small. Behind a glass partition about half the height of the wall two barbers were working by their chairs. Five or six Jews were sitting in the anteroom, its one window and little round table both covered by a kind of green, plush cloth. The men were all shaved. As I found out later they only shaved at home, but Sundays they'd come here anyway, just to sit. Their ages were different, but their loneliness was the same. They'd all had families before the war, but not after. That's the kind of luck a Jew would have: If he was at the Front he stood a better chance of surviving than the family he'd left behind.

They suffered from the same misfortune. All week long it was work, work, work, and when their day off came it found them sad and lonely. Crying didn't help so they sought each other out.

They could have met at a café of course. But they didn't drink, and it's not right to sit in a café if you don't. Besides, there'd be a lot of people there and it wouldn't be so cozy. Anyway, it cost money.

But here at The Road to Happiness barbershop you could sit all day with your own people talking about whatever you liked without bothering a soul. It was like being at home. And if a stranger came all you'd have to do was tell him to go straight to the chair without waiting because you'd shaved already. And if the chair was busy that wouldn't be so bad either. You could listen to somebody new and—who knows?—that could be interesting, too.

I'd go to The Road to Happiness every Sunday and always find the same crowd. I'd take a seat beside them and we'd talk. Pretty soon they got used to me, asked about the details of my life, and began to consider me one of their own.

And I listened. The stories they told me I'd like to pass on to you now. Maybe they'll interest you as much as they once did me.

So, seeing we're agreed, I'll begin.

Story of Why Rabbi Arn Respects the Germans, As Told By Himself

Rabbi Arn. That's what they called him here in the barbershop, and I'm sure they had no other name. He was years older than the rest. Short and stout, he had a sizable belly with an old-fashioned pair of colored suspenders stretched tight across it. He suffered from shortness of breath, and he'd always take his jacket off the second he arrived. Rabbi Arn puffed on a cigar that was fat, brown, and usually out. In some ways he looked a lot like it himself. Maybe it was those red eyebrows and whitish lashes that did it or that fat, deeply creased face with the same kind of brown dots on it that covered his vast bald spot.

Rabbi Arn didn't say much and mostly listened. When he did, you had a hard time telling if he was interested or not. Those watery eyes of his would give a dim look from under the whitish lashes and what lay hidden behind them was anybody's guess. He was held in high esteem here, and every Sunday they'd wait for him to come before getting under way.

He'd spend a long time lighting his cigar, puffing with a whistle while his head turned crimson from the strain, and everybody would wait respectfully for his torments to end. The moment would come, the cigar would start to smolder, and they'd all sigh with relief, leaning back, like him, into their chairs.

"I'll tell you what I respect the Germans for," said Rabbi Arn at last, his cigar lighted and a cloud of smelly smoke curling around him. "They're punctual."

A start like that made the group perk up all right. So what's this? Rabbi Arn, of all people, talking about respecting the Germans? Listen to that, will you? And he's not the type to say a word for nothing, either. Well, let's see what he's driving at.

"When the Germans were cleaning up the last of the Jews— a half a year this was after they'd shot all the women and children—they had us men working on road repair. From the side we'd already fixed, the murder bus would pull up. You know the kind I mean. The same sort of panel truck they carry bread in nowadays. An iron door in back and two little steps. Quiet as a mouse it would drive up to you and swing its rear end around. Then the soldiers would open the door and an officer would count out the ten or twelve closest to the bus. 'Lay down your picks and shovels,' he'd tell them, 'neatly.' Then he'd invite them to step into the wagon one at a time. Up they'd go, the soldiers would close the doors, and the van would take off. Meanwhile, we'd keep on working like nothing had happened. Until the wagon came back. Empty. And the pile of abandoned picks and shovels by the road would grow and grow.

"In case somebody still doesn't get it, I'll give a little clue. On its run from us to a big anti-tank ditch in the woods the wagon was pumping its exhaust right into the closed part where the people were. By the time they'd open the door at the ditch, everybody inside would be dead as a doornail already—and pure blue, too, as they say.

"We keep on working, the wagon comes and goes, and there's fewer and fewer of us left on the road. I take a look. I'm on the edge already, five or six people ahead of me. That means my trip's next. The mathematics of it isn't hard.

"I'm next. So, I'm next. I can change my place, maybe, and move back a bit if I'm quiet about it. That way I'll put the whole

22

thing off by one trip and then what? Swing my pick a little longer? Who needs it?

"I look and it's coming. An officer counts us out. I carry my pick over to the pile and line up. One thing more I have to tell you. You had to climb into the wagon one at a time, single file. Order—the Germans are crazy about it. First up goes one, then another. I was around the sixth or seventh. I admit it, there was an ugly smell coming from the open door of the wagon and it was all I could think about. Just that smell.

"The officer stands by the bottom step, counts us off as we go in, and keeps an eye glued to his wristwatch. I had one foot on the step already when suddenly he dropped his hand and gave a yell. '*Ap! Zwölft Uhr! Mittagessen!*' 'That's it!' he says. 'Twelve o'clock! Dinnertime!'

"I took my foot off the step, they slammed the doors shut, and off went the wagon without a full load."

For a long while Rabbi Arn looked at the smoldering tip of his cigar. It was covered with a gray, unbroken ash, and he concluded:

"I'll tell you what I respect the Germans for. They're punctual."

Then he gave us a look with those watery eyes and whitish lashes. As for what was on his mind, you wouldn't find a clue to save your life.

Story of an Unpleasant Character and His Saintly Wife, As Told By a Man Whose Name I Do Not Know

"Now listen to what happened in our town. Unique is the term for it. I wouldn't have believed it myself if there hadn't been eyewitnesses. Living ones, of course, not Jews. Them you'd have to get from the Other World.

"So anyway, listen. And no interruptions. I told this story someplace else already, and a doctor was there and he said to me, 'Pure fantasy, things like that don't happen,' he says. Now I'm no doctor and as for medicine all I know is what hurts and what doesn't. But doctors nowadays, take my word for it, they know even less. What's written in books, that they know, but what happens in real life, they don't want to know. All right, let it pass. Let them doctor from books if it makes them happy and cripple people for all I care, I only know one thing: Life's richer than fantasy. So don't be like that doctor and don't interrupt.

"Now then, what was I going to tell you? Oh, yes.

"In our *shtetl* there lived a Jew. I know, you're going to pop up and tell me, 'And he discovered America, right?' So who lives in a *shtetl* besides Jews? True. But this Jew wasn't like the others, although the way things are going nowadays, God only knows who's a Jew and who isn't.

"Moishe they called this one. A blacksmith. Forged horseshoes, made nails, fitted wheels. A blacksmith like any other. What else is there to do in a small town? And I won't deny it, he

24

was a good blacksmith, first-class. Say they'd bring him a jumpy horse, kicking like a madman, even the peasant who owns it is scared. And Moishe? Well, he gives that horse such a look and such a holler—he had a throat like cast iron and I'll tell you why in a minute—that the horse just stands there flabbergasted, like an obedient child, and Moishe drives the nails into its hoofs.

"As for the cast-iron throat, the reason why is no secret. Moishe never once opened the shop without taking a thick shot of vodka. And for lunch, the same thing, without a bite to eat even. Just a sleeve across his lips, wipe, wipe. What kind of a Jew would let something like that happen to him? I told you, he wasn't like the rest. And as for the others they just stayed away. A pure *goy* this was. Couldn't drag him to *shul* with a rope. And yet he wasn't a day under seventy, we should live so long. He didn't talk much, but when he did everybody would hightail it, not only people in their right mind—horses, too. One thing I have to tell you. Moishe had been a soldier in the Czar's army back in the war with the Japanese. That's where he learned how to talk Russian. And he swore such a blue streak in it that the old folks used to say, next to him even a policeman was sweet as a kitten's breath.

"I told you already, this was no regular Jew, and people who didn't have business with him wouldn't even say hello. Dark, bearded, gloomy as a thundercloud, a smell of coal and vodka on him it would cut you down from a mile away. To live with him in the same house would be a very small pleasure. Even if they paid you extra, who'd agree to it?

"But there was one creature who took it all like a saint. Toiba, his wife.* A dove, I'm telling you, in every sense of the word. Small, quiet, and kind. Wouldn't hurt a fly. Tender and sweet

* *Toib:* in Yiddish, a dove.

to everybody. And always a smile on her face. She lived her whole life with him, can you imagine? Had seven sons, too, big as oxen like Moishe. Only a little smarter, it's true. All seven grew up and went their separate ways, some to America, some to Russia, one to Brazil even.

"And in their home in the little town there were seven portraits on the wall. Otherwise, the place was empty and lonely as a beggar's purse. The only time there'd be noise was when Moishe had had one too many. Then you could hear the dishes crashing to the floor. People would go a little faster past their windows at times like that, mourning for the poor, unhappy Toiba in their hearts. There was something frightening about this man, all right, a husband like you'd wish only on your worst enemy. That is, if you were heartless yourself.

"This you won't believe, but never once did she complain about him to anyone and never, God forbid, did she visit a single curse on his head. Just the opposite. From her you could hear only the best; to listen to her, he was a saint.

"Where's that doctor now who interrupted me. I'd like to see his books make sense out of something like that.

"True, Moishe never once laid a finger on his Toiba. That's all he had to do. A punch from him could kill a horse, so there must have been something of the Jew in him after all.

"Anyway, that's the way it went. The women feared Moishe and pitied Toiba. They could be glad of their own husbands, at least. They could live with them without fear, even shout at them sometimes. You know what our wives were like, they'd give up bread if you gave them a chance to holler. Otherwise life wasn't life.

"Our poor wives, may they rest in peace, *that* they knew how to do. How they loved it.

"Anyway, Toiba took it all in stride, humbly, whatever God

26

sent her way, it was her lot. But a human heart is no rock. There's a limit to everything. One fine day she had a stroke.

"You can imagine for yourself what it's like to lie paralyzed in bed day after day for three long years waiting for a man like Moishe to come lift a spoon to your mouth. Better drop dead there and then and have done with it. But God has different ideas. And so Toiba would lie in an empty house, as alone as could be, look at the pictures of her sons, and ask God to let her die. As for Moishe, he'd hammer away all day long at the shop and swear his heart out. He'd get home late, cook up some kind of soup on the stove, toss off a glass of vodka, and like an animal looking sideways at the floor, start to feed Toiba with a spoon. You know, it would have been better never to have seen that feeding at all. The tenderest words he could say to his wife were 'You skunk.' I'm sorry, but it's the truth I'm telling you, and you have to be frank. What are you going to do, that's the kind of man he was. Maybe he wanted to say something nicer. It wouldn't come out. You know the saying: 'Toads on his tongue.'

"He'd be shoeing a horse. All of a sudden, bam! he'd give it such a hit on the withers it would stagger back and then, to the horse or just himself maybe, he'd say, 'Okay, that's it. I'm going to feed the skunk.'

"Such a breadwinner, if you can call him that, you'd wish only on your enemies.

"A year passes, then another, and Toiba doesn't die. Out of spite, you'd think. Moishe hammers away in the shop all day and every morning and every evening he feeds her with a spoon. Curses for all he's worth, but he does the laundry himself and even washes his old lady. Nobody ever saw it, but women who'd drop by to visit would always find her clean and neatly dressed. And the house all tidy. Not even a smudge on the floor.

"Now here comes the main part of the story. The war. By the

second day the Germans were already drawing near the town. The Jews took to their heels. They caught up their children in their arms and threw all their belongings to the wind, just to get the hell out. Anything to put a little distance on the Germans.

"They ran past the shop and heard the blacksmith pounding. They glanced in and cried:

"'Moishe! Are you crazy? Everybody's running. Ditch it! The Germans are coming!'

"He kept on hammering and didn't even look.

"'Moishe! Are you listening? The Germans! Run with us, they'll kill you here!'

"He lay down the hammer and gave them a look.

"'And who'll take care of the skunk?'

"Do you understand? He didn't go. For Toiba he stayed. Others, the holiest of holies, were abandoning their old and sick, whoever couldn't make it on foot, and taking to their heels themselves. But Moishe stayed. The drunk, the nobody, the scoundrel, the thug. Nobody in town could think of a better word for him. He didn't leave with the rest. For another day or two, while there was work, he hammered away at the thop. Then he locked himself in with Toiba and didn't leave. He sat there by her bed, feeding her with a spoon, and abusing her with all his heart. Skunk was the most endearing term he used.

"The cleanup began, and the police started ransacking all the Jewish homes. When they got to Moishe's, Toiba was lying paralyzed in bed, looking tenderly at her husband like he was a child. They ordered him to get up and he stood. He looked at his old lady and said good-by with his eyes. When suddenly she began to stir. Do you understand what I'm saying? Three whole years and not a single movement. And then, out of the blue, she sits up. She looks at her husband and at the Germans and smiles.

"'Wait,' she says, although to this moment her tongue hasn't moved for three years. 'Don't take him alone. I'm going with him.'

"And she stood up! As if there'd never been a trace of paralysis. She walked up to her husband and smiled. Arm in arm they went, the way it used to be long, long ago when they were young. And together they left. And together, arm in arm, they stood by the edge of the grave, Toiba looking at him with love in her eyes. And together, their arms around each other, they dropped into the hole when the bullets flew.

"And the doctor says . . . What does *he* have to say? What do any of these doctors know of life?"

Story of the Good People Still Left in This World, As Told By a Person Whose Name I Don't Know Either

" 'I've come to you as a Jew.'

"Now picture my situation for a minute. That's all I needed to hear. I'm hanging by a thread. Every morning I expect them to give me the sack. I mean I hold one of the leading posts on the job. Large or small, that's another matter, but a position of importance all the same. I'm in charge of an artel of invalids. You can understand, it's not a factory, it's an ache at heart. We make toothbrushes out of pig bristles. And my workers? One without an eye, another without a hand, a third without a leg. And almost all of them shell shocked. Say one word to them and you get back ten. Even pitch a crutch at you. You tell *me* how much work you can expect to get out of them. Don't make me laugh. And every month they boost the quota—and every month we fill it. How? Beats me, but we slither out. What choice have we got anyway? If we don't make it, they kick me out. So my invalids hold on to me. One hand washes the other, we both keep each other alive. If I were to get fired, they'd have to go begging. And the same goes for me. Without a right hand what can I do? Supervise, that's all. And where are you going to find a Jew in that kind of position nowadays?

"So, to cut it short, I sit quiet as a mouse, I meet the quota, and I try to stay out of the limelight. Nowadays my nose isn't too stylish. I better not stick it where it doesn't belong.

"Then this woman comes into my office. A Lithuanian. 'I've

come to you,' she says, 'as a Jew.' Words that put me in a cold sweat, I tell you.

"She sat down and looked me in the eye with the kind of expression you only see on Jews. I even thought for a second maybe she's a Jew too, but no, a hundred per cent Lithuanian and still she's got that Jewish look. Why? Because she'd stepped into our shoes for a minute. You meet a lot of very good people among the Lithuanians all right, and she was one of them. Listen to what she said.

"She lived with her husband and kids in a little town somewhere in Zhemaitiya. I don't even remember what it was he did. Something or other. Simple people. Barely enough to live on. But their home was their own and so was the cow. That's the way they lived.

"One day, under the Germans this was, a column of Jews was being driven down the street to be shot. The Lithuanians locked themselves up in their homes. Who'd want to watch a thing like that anyway? Well, this woman forgot to close her gate.

"When the column was passing her house one of the Jews pushed her children through the open gate. A boy and a girl. And on she went with the rest of the column without even looking back.

"The Jews passed and the Lithuanian went outside to her yard. And there she sees them, those two abandoned children, the poor things, squatting on the grass and crying. The Lithuanian looks at them and realizes what a misfortune's just hit her from the blue. Everybody knows you get shot for harboring Jews. She had no choice; it was grab the kids and take them back to the Germans. To tell you the truth that's what she wanted to do at first. She admitted it to me. She even grabbed them by the hand. But when she felt those little hands in hers

31

and saw how trustingly they gave them to her, it wrung her heart. She was a mother herself, you know, and she just couldn't do it. In a fog she closed the gate quick so nobody else could see and inform on her, and she took the kids into the house. She washed them and she fed them. Then, very strictly, she ordered them to keep silent and, neither dead nor alive, she waits for her husband to get back home from work. How is she going to explain it? What's he going to say? Giving those kids back to the Germans is totally out of the question by now. She's washed them already and fed them with her own hands. . . . What if her husband refuses? . . . She'd brought a terrible misfortune into the house, all right. On account of those kids her own might have to die.

"It was then, I think, that Jewish look came into her eyes.

"Her husband returned from work. She gave him something to eat. When it was completely dark she led him to the larder, unlocked it, and with a candle in her hand showed him the Jewish boy and girl asleep on a little bast mat. The husband understood everything. For a long time he just looked. Didn't say a word. Then he locked the storeroom and went off to bed. All night long he tossed and he groaned, but he didn't say a word.

"What a misfortune for that family. Now there were four children to feed instead of two. The husband started working evenings, she took in other people's wash. But the main thing—and it never let up—was the fear. What if the Germans suddenly caught on? Or the neighbors informed on them? The kids were living things, you know, you couldn't keep them under lock and key all the time. And then what about their own? They were young and they might happen to say something. Life? No, this was a nightmare.

"Finally somebody did get wind. A little rumor began to

spread. It was a small town, everybody knew what was stewing in everybody else's pot. Two kids, they're no needle in a haystack. The end was drawing near.

"That's when they ran. For next to nothing they sold their house and stole away in the night. Clear to the other end of Lithuania where nobody knew them. They bought some kind of shack to live in. All over again they started their lives and hid their misfortune: the two Jewish children fate had tossed their way. And for how long this time? Only until somebody here figured out who they were hiding.

"Again they had to throw it all away. Again they had to make a new home someplace else. God only knows how they lasted till the Soviet Army came, but they did, they survived, and they saved the kids. Kids who were like their own to them by now.

"Well, they thought, our troubles are finally over. They didn't expect any thanks for what they'd done. It was just a good deed and now they could start living a life in peace.

"That wasn't to be. They were simple people, they didn't understand a thing about politics, and they acted straight from their hearts. They registered both kids as Jews and gave them back their real names, thinking that if their relatives suddenly cropped up, they'd be able to find them. They wanted nothing but the best, but it turned out all wrong. For them and for the kids.

"The children grew up. It was time to set them up in life. But where? They were Jews after all. Who'd take them? What could they do?

"And so the poor Lithuanian goes her way, haunting thresholds. To this day she's still as tormented with those abandoned kids as a hen with ducklings. That's why she says to me, 'I've come to you as a Jew. Help me set up my children. With the boy everything's settled for the time being. They took him into

the Army. But what about the girl? They won't take her anywhere. Help me get her a job. You're a Jew, you must understand.'

"That's what she tells me, this Lithuanian, and she looks at
me with that expression I used to find only on Jews."

Story of
How Yasha Looked Three Weeks for a Field Hospital, As Told By Himself

"Jews, give a listen. There aren't any customers, and Mirra hasn't come yet, so I'll tell you a story. It'll make you laugh those sad looks right off your faces."

Said Yasha, the barber, putting his scissors and comb into the breast pocket of his monogrammed white coat.

Yasha's always been a smiler. His thick lips smile, his broad nose smiles, his bulging eyes, like a crab's, they smile. Even his thick curly head of hair smiles.

Yasha doesn't have a tooth to call his own. Both jaws are packed with big, glittering metal teeth. All he has to do is open those thick, inflated lips of his and this unbearable glitter lights up his high round cheekbones like a smile. It gives him a perpetually good-natured look, which some people take for a sign of idiocy. But Yasha's no fool. Far from it. You have my word.

Take that jacket of his, for example, the one always hanging on a nail near the mirror in front of the barber chair. Any other person would have hung his jacket up on the stand in the ante-room. Not Yasha; he keeps his jacket right where he works, as a big eyesore for his customers. That's right, eyesore. Oy, Yasha, he's no fool!

Three decorations and five medals hang on Yasha's coat. Hang and glitter. Not that they ask for trouble, but a customer, even the most inveterate anti-Semite, would sooner swallow his tongue than offend Yasha with a careless remark. Sure he's only a barber and a Jew, but he's a war veteran too with all those decorations and medals. Who knows? He's got a good-natured face, but what he might do to you, you never can tell. Better not get involved.

So they don't. The customers in Yasha's chair would smile even if he stuffed their mouths full of shaving cream. Yasha smiles, the customer smiles, and the medals? How they gleam!

His partner, the old man Borukhovich, emaciated as a telephone pole, his bald head flattened on the sides and crowned with sparse white tufts like some exotic bird, openly despises Yasha. Because Yasha has so many medals and he doesn't have any; because Yasha is always smiling and he, as you'd expect from a serious master, is always sullen and tight-lipped; and mainly because Yasha is the only man in the barbershop with a family of his own: a wife, Mirra, whom Borukhovich also detests, and children.

Borukhovich despises the whole world. It all started after a stay at Osventsim. By the time they pulled him out of there he was a walking corpse. His wife and children stayed behind, in the crematorium, as big piles of ashes. Since then for some reason he's suspected everyone of a lack of culture and tries to rub shoulders as little as possible. He shaves and is silent. He cuts hair and won't say a word. At every joke to come along he shrugs his shoulders. And when they ask him why, he answers he's accustomed to associating only with cultured people. Although even the word "cultured" he pronounces like an illiterate, with some accent from God knows where. *"Khultured,"** he says.

Borukhovich especially despises Yasha for the thanks customers sometimes write for Yasha in the "Book of Complaints and Suggestions" and never for him. And this in spite of the fact

---

* Russian *intèllikhèntnyi.*

that Borukhovich was a master, first-class; why, before the war, in Kovno, people used to line up to make appointments with him and they even had a telephone in the shop.

"Look out the window. Mirra isn't coming, is she?" asked Yasha. When they'd all turned their heads to the window and assured him that Mirra wasn't, Yasha began his tale.

"As far as I can tell, there's nobody here from the Sixteenth Division, right? Otherwise, he'd have a chest full of medals. You couldn't stay alive in the Sixteenth and not get decorated, that was out of the question. Besides, I'd know him personally. I knew all the Jews in the Sixteenth and, aside from Jews, who else was there? Anyway, I've told you already, anyone who'd ever been in the Sixteenth had what you could call an insolent expression. Not that he was really insolent, but he'd pulled through alive and he still couldn't believe it.

"It should come as no surprise they didn't make the Division because Lithuanian Jews were dying to fight. It was a lot simpler than that. Lithuanians weren't running from the Germans. In fact, the only people in the whole country to take to their heels were the Jews. So when the time came to form a Lithuanian Division for the Soviet Army, this one, the Sixteenth, they rummaged through all of Russia and the only Lithuanians they could come up with were Jews.

"They grouped us on the Volga, in Balakhna. Anybody here ever been there? Don't worry, you didn't miss much. Only nice thing about it was the women. Mirra isn't coming, is she? I'm telling you, the women there were out of this world. That was something only the officers got to appreciate, though. They drilled us and exercised us from morning till night. We'd come crawling back to the barracks on all fours. You can guess what we had in mind by then.

"Anyway, the Division set off for the Front. They put Russian officers in command, a couple of Jews, and a Lithuanian and a half. From Siberia this was. Those guys were about as Lithuanian as I am. Only worse. They knew two words in Lithuanian. And with such an accent that, compared to them, I was Kipras Petrauskas.†

"In all the official documents they called the Division the Sixteenth Lithuanian. We called it the Lithuanian Jewish Division, though, and all the way to the Front the only songs the column sang were Jewish. There just weren't any Jewish marching songs and the standard Russian ones we didn't know. It's like a law in Russia: When you march you've got to sing. For spiritual uplift. You know, to keep your pants up. So we'd sing 'Afn Pripechek Brent a Faerl'‡ or 'Ven der Rebbeh Ele-Meilakh iz Gevorn zeyer Freilakh.'** It was a lot easier dancing to those songs than marching, so whenever we'd pass by the generals we'd go into this song somebody or other had dreamed up. That, at least, you could march to. I still remember the words:

> *'Marsh, marsh, marsh. Ich gei in bod.*
> *Krats mich ois di pleitseh.*
> *Nein, nein, nein. Ich vil nicht gein.*
> *A dank dich far der eitseh.'*††

"The generals wouldn't get a word of it and they'd praise us as we passed. 'Fine lads, those Lithuanians! Great songs!'

"We kept on singing till we came under fire. That's when it really opened up. The works, all right! The Orlovsky-Kursk Bulge. Ever hear of it? It was hell. Nowadays even the books

† Kipras Petrauskas: a well-known Lithuanian artist.
‡ "A Little Fire's Burning in the Oven."
** "When Rabbi Ele-Meilakh Kicked Up His Heels."
†† "March, march, march. I'm going to the steam house.
  Scratch me on the back.
  No, no, no. I don't want to go.
  Thanks for the advice."

say there wasn't any other fighting like it in the whole war. We were lucky if there was even a fifth of the Division left. Later in the papers they talked about great feats and heroic deeds. Maybe from their angle you could see things better.

"Anyway that's beside the point. They took us back behind the lines for rest and reinforcement. And where were you going to get reinforcements for a Lithuanian Division when there weren't any Lithuanians in Russia? You got it. They started looking for Lithuanian Jews again. Old ones, sick ones, and cripples. Reinforcements arrived all right, and the first thing I wanted to do when I saw them was go hang myself.

"I'd been the commanding officer of a mortar unit and the only one in it to come out alive. So I got the reinforcements. Jews come in all kinds, but they gave the real winners to me. *Shlimazl* on *shlimazl*. Not just from any old place, either, but Panevezhis itself."‡‡

"From Panevezhis he wants *khultured* people," taunted Borukhovich over his shoulder, pointing his razor at Yasha. To look at him, though, shaving his customer with such diligence, you'd have thought he hadn't been listening at all.

"On the nose!" said Yasha. "You had to see this to believe it. Shoemakers at the end of their rope, tailors, barbers. A mortar shell? They hadn't even held a rifle in their hands! The *tsuris* I had with them? I'd swear at them in Russian till I turned blue in the face. Nothing helped. They just went to pieces. They'd hold a shell by the tips of their fingers like it was a dead mouse and poke it in the barrel the wrong way. I knew it. My end had come. If the Germans didn't get me first my Panevezhis reinforcements were going to blow the whole battery up for sure and I'd be knocked sky high even before my first order to open fire.

"God had mercy. I don't know how, but we reached the Front

‡‡ Panevezhis: a little town in Lithuania.

without being blown up. Somehow I got them into battle formation and waited to see what would happen when we opened fire.
Something good, of course, I don't expect. But maybe God
would take pity and send me a quick and painless death.

"Luckily the Germans started shooting first. They blasted us
from six-barreled guns and covered my unit. Didn't even catch
one of my Panevezhis recruits. A miracle this was: Those boys
really had learned to dig in. The only fragment hit me, right in
the hand. You know that when you're hit you don't feel it at first,
you just see the blood. Well, when I saw it gushing out of my
hand I was so happy I nearly wept for joy. That's it! I'm saved!
My Panevezhis boys can't blow me up now! I'm wounded and
by law my place is in the field hospital. The only trouble is you
have to know where things are at the Front. Go find the field
hospital yourself in the middle of a battle with the Germans
leading an artillery attack all over the place. You'd have better
luck chasing the wind in the fields. So, off I went to look. My
blood's pouring out, shells and mines are going off all around
me, and I'm smiling with happiness. You could have taken me
for a lunatic if you didn't know where I was coming from or
what kind of miracle had just saved me from my boys.

"I look here, I look there, and there's no field hospital. If only
I'd met a single living medic. But I told you already; you have
to know where things are at the Front. I'd already gone a few
kilometers when I saw a village. And nothing there but women.
Anyone here ever been to the Orlovsky region? Take a look out
the window, Mirra isn't coming, is she? Let me tell you, the
women there they'd make you rock and reel. They bandaged
my hand, fed me, bathed me like a child. You've really never
been to Orlovsky? You've missed a lot.

"I stayed with those women like an earl, for two or three days.
And what days, what days! Mirra isn't coming? What could I

possibly tell you? But I knew it, time to quit, time to go looking for the field hospital again.

"I moved on. Where's the field hospital? What field hospital? I came to another village. Believe me, I'm really sorry for you. The women in Orlovsky! Oy, is that Mirra coming? No? You're sure? Then I'll tell you a little more.

"It wasn't life I found in that second village—it was a bowl full of cherries. I got myself a woman there—how can words do justice? A whole week flew by and I didn't even notice.

"All the same I had to find the field hospital. I moved on. I look and there's another village. Jews, listen to me. If you haven't been to Orlovsky what's there to talk about?

"By the time I found the field hospital, after the third village this was, there wasn't even a trace left of my wound. All healed. Just this scar left, on both sides. The thing had gone clear through. My teeth got knocked out later, in East Prussia."

Yasha rolled up his coat sleeve and showed us his hairy hand. There was the crimson track of a wound on it, like the seam from an electric welder. The Jews all moved in for a closer look. Franya even smelled it for some reason. Borukhovich was the only one not to leave his chair. Diligent as could be, he kept on shaving his customer, even though he did squint over the top of his glasses.

"They just about called me a deserter at the field hospital." Yasha burst out laughing. "Sent me right back to the Front the same day, too. And where do you think? To my dear old Lithuanian Division. I got there right after some heavy fighting and none of the men I knew had been left alive. As for my mortar unit, those miserable Panevezhis boys, not even a whiff left. I had to wait for reinforcements again. . . . That was a big laugh, all right. . . ."

What kind of laugh Yasha couldn't say. A customer had entered, the Jews let him pass without waiting, and Yasha went to the chair to strop his razor, still smiling and shaking his thick, curly head.

No one paid him any attention when he entered the barbershop. A Jew like any other, small and unspectacular. If there was anything striking about that face it was the large, bulging eyes, a trace of guilt in them maybe, and the soft, hanging nose. But eyes like that are nothing special among Jews and certainly not that kind of nose. The only thing worth noticing was his baggy cloak, an ivory-colored affair with shoulder straps and yoke, and hemispheres of braided leather buttons. A foreign cut, all right, nothing local about it.

They all gave it a look while he wore it and even after, when he hung it bashfully on the stand and got out of the warm underlining of synthetic fur. As for what the cloak left behind, the owner himself, he quietly took a seat at the very edge of the free chair and nobody could have cared less. He looked meekly at everybody and didn't even dare ask who was last in line. The group had already decided to return to its previous occupation—talking.

But then somebody's glance, slipping lazily across him, happened to linger in bewilderment. And then another and another. Now they were all looking.

The left side of his narrow little jacket was covered with a bright, multicolored patch. It was splendid: three rows of military citations of the most amazing colors and sizes. And not one that looked even the slightest bit Russian. You could tell they were all foreign.

None of this squared with the rest of his appearance as a quiet, provincial Jew from somewhere out in Ukmere or Pakalnishek. The sight of those foreign decorations drove everyone crazy with curiosity. They started fidgeting and scraping their chairs, sighing and coughing, not knowing what angle to come at him from.

So many intrigued glances on him, and all the man could do was gaze at the floor and mince his delicate thin fingers on his knees.

"*Vos tut a Yid?*"

With this traditional question, familiar to Jews on all continents, Rabbi Arn finally let the steam out.

The man flinched. When he realized the question was for him, he smiled sadly and trustingly.

"You're going to laugh," he said, "but I'm looking for Mama."

As a matter of fact behind the register Franya did burst out laughing into her fist. The others coughed so loud you'd have thought they were choking to death. Rabbi Arn was the only one to keep quiet. Nothing surprised him any more. "Well, any luck?" he inquired politely.

"*Proszę pana?*" the man excused himself in Polish, raising himself a little in his chair.

Rabbi Arn repeated the question.

"That's just it, I haven't found her." The smile was gone from his face. He spread his arms in a helpless gesture, like an offended child.

By now everybody was ready to explode with curiosity. The scent of a fresh story filled the barbershop.

"Listen, will you stop tormenting us?" They turned to him. "Tell us everything. In order, from start to finish."

"Well, if you're sure I'm not taking up your time . . ."

"Time we've got plenty of," Rabbi Arn spoke for all. "It's Sunday."

Story of How a Son Searched for His Mama All Through the War, As Told By Yankel, Known Also As Yan, John, and Jean Lapidus, a Stateless Person With a Residence Permit

"*Przepraszam,** my Russian is bad and I ask your forgiveness in advance. I was born here at Vilno, under Poland, and now I come and it's Lithuania. And Mama and I lived on Pogulianka Street and now it's Donelaitis Street and our home is gone from there, while a new one's built. And from the neighbors we had I didn't find anybody. If someone lived in Vilno before the war under the Polish, then maybe he remembers my mama. Pani Lapidus. That's what they called her, because she had a *sklep*† and on the *shield*‡ it was written 'Hot Bagels. Madam Lapidus and Son.' But even if I was on the sign, I wasn't in the shop. I was at the *Gymnasium* studying and Mama wanted me to finish university and become a lawyer very much. She worked for this day and night. Everything she did herself. She kneaded the dough and she baked and she sold, all herself. While I studied. And in 1939 exactly I finished Gymnasium with honors. My poor mama cried with the joy three days and three nights because her hardships weren't in vain and her son made all her hopes come true.

"In my eyes, *przepraszam*, when I speak of my poor mama there are always tears. So don't you pay attention. Mama loved me very much and I also. I could not live without her. It was

---

* "Excuse me," in Polish.
† Shop.
‡ Sign.

just the two of us in the whole wide world. My father I don't remember. Just Mama and me. We always lived the two of us together and I didn't know how I would go to the university in Warsaw. How will I stay without Mama and Mama without me?

"But Mama wanted only one thing, for her son to go to the capital and get a Warsaw diploma. So in the summer of '39 I went, and we both were wet from the tears when we said good-by at the Vilno train station. Now I think our hearts were telling us the same thing: Good-by, we are seeing each other for the very last time. *Przepraszam*. May I smoke? . . .

"So. In Warsaw I passed the examinations in all the subjects, but the money Mama gave me for the trip was all spent. Because the next day I called her from Warsaw on the trunk line and summoned her to the trunk call office, which cost very much. But I missed her so I was afraid to fail on the examinations if I didn't hear her voice again. It's not easy for me to talk about this, for I am a man and here I could not live a day without my mama. Before the war people loved their mamas more than now in general. That's what all the people say.

"The first of September I was to go to the university for the first time as a student and I received a telegram of congratulations from Mama. *Przepraszam*. This was the last telegram from her I got.

"On that day Germany attacked Poland and, as you know, the Second World War was started. I was very disturbed, because the war is going on and I am in Warsaw but Mama is in Vilno. And she too, it must be. At such times it is best of all to be together. Especially for me and my mama.

"But I received a notice. They were calling me into the Polish Army. I wanted to call Mama, but with Vilno there was no connection any more. What kind of soldier they could make with me you see for yourself. But they were taking everybody, and they took me. They dressed me in an army coat, they tossed a cap with a white eagle on my head, and they started to teach us on the parade ground how to march. They said rifles we give you later, when it's time to fight.

"Now the Germans started to bomb Warsaw, it was all on fire and there was panic. They said that tanks were already coming close to Visla. The officers scattered and they ordered us to go to our homes. But where is my home? My home is in Vilno, on Pogulianka Street. So I went. On foot. With the refugees headed for the East. That was the way to Vilno. And ever since then I have been looking for my mama.

"I didn't get to Vilno. The Soviets, the Red Army, attacked Poland from behind and we all fell into the hands of the Russians. *Przepraszam*, I forgot to tell you that I was wearing the military clothes I was dismissed in to go home. The Russians noticed me and they didn't let me by as a refugee; they took me prisoner, me, a student in an army coat and a cap with a white eagle. Why I didn't throw this coat and this cap along the road I don't know myself. The overcoat was of good cloth and I thought to myself, if the cloth is dyed it will make Mama a winter coat. I did not want to come home with my hands empty.

"I cried, I asked them to let me go to Vilno, that it was very near, to see my mama, and then they can do with me what they want. The Russian officer didn't understand Polish, or he didn't want to hear me. So, they carried me off in a cattle car with the other Polish captured, past Vilno and straight to Siberia we went.

"There in the taiga we stayed in wooden barracks behind barbed wire, without the right to get letters or send them, and I couldn't even eat, I suffered so. They made us work, too, sawing down trees. This was good. Because when you are tired and there is buzzing in your arms and legs, you don't think about your fate so much.

"For me it was worse than the others. I didn't know how to saw wood, I made a mess of things and the guards would swear at me. The Poles would mock me, too, because there were anti-Semites with them and they didn't like Jews. It was hard all around and I didn't know what I was suffering for. But the main thing was I didn't know anything about what was happening to Mama. The only thing we knew was that Vilno had been taken by the Russians and handed over to the Lithuanians who called it by a different name, Vilnyus. But whether she was there, or where she was, nothing. And she must be going crazy thinking that I have fallen into German hands and died.

"I was alive, freezing to death in Siberia behind the barbed wire, and I suffered all kinds of mockery and I wanted to die very much. But first I had to see Mama, even if with one eye only.

"I won't make the story long, you will be bored. Soon the Germans attacked Russia and we became allies with the Russians. From the prisoners of war they made a Polish Army with General Anders in command. And that's where I went. They let us out from behind the barbed wire, they dressed us in everything new, again with the white eagle, they gave us good rations, and for the first time I was given a rifle, which before this I had never held in my hands.

"I shot so poorly in the training exercises that our Under-Ensign Pan Boreisha called me a Kike snout and took away my rifle. He ordered them to give me a machine gun. Because you can shoot one of them without aiming and to learn it you must be educated. Besides, Pan Boreisha said that a machine gun was heavier than a rifle, so let the Jew carry it on his back.

"Yes. The machine gun was heavy and I had a lot to endure from it. It scraped my back until the blood came.

"They put us on a troop train and carried us through Russia, clear across. On the road I sent five letters to Vilno, but all in vain. The Germans had taken Vilno and were already near Moscow.

"We thought they're taking us to the Front, but no, it turned out they weren't. General Anders had outwitted the Russians, and our Polish Army crossed through Iran, Persia that is, to join the English in Africa. Anders didn't like the Bolsheviks at all, and for us it was all the same where we died: in the snow near Moscow or in the sand near Tobruk.

"*Przepraszam*, have you heard the name, Tobruk? Thank God you haven't. The heaviest fighting in Africa, that was. Not with the Italians, either, that would have been a pleasure, but with real Germans from Rommel's army. And of course the English threw us right into the fire, right into hell. They felt sorry for their own soldiers, but not for the Poles.

"It's the truth, *proszę pana*. God's truth. Ask any Pole who was left alive after Tobruk. It was very hard on us. Hot, hardly any water, the Germans bombing us. At one point I started to go deaf. For that I got the English Order of the Cross of Victoria, this one here. You laugh. God's truth. If it won't bore you, I can tell you the story.

"Our battalion had taken a position near Tobruk. A bare wilderness this was, with nowhere to hide. The soil was so rocky it was very hard to dig a trench. There, where we were lying, was the intersection of two roads. One went away from the Germans into Tobruk, the other crossed it perpendicularly, and it was here we took up a defensive position. Right where the roads crossed a concrete pipe had been laid beneath the ground. This was in case it rained, to drain out the water. But it was dry then, 'so I carried my machine gun into it, because I didn't have the strength to dig the emplacement, and I pointed the muzzle outside.

"To the right of me lies our battalion, and to the left, from the other end of the pipe, still another battalion, also Poles. I look: From the right, where I'm lying, the Germans are coming at us. I must shoot, I think. I don't hear the order to fire because I've gone deaf, but if I don't shoot, then Under-Ensign Pan Boreisha will strike me in the face for being a coward.

"So I started shooting, wherever, without sticking my head outside the pipe, until I used up the whole magazine. I leaned out to see what's happening; the Germans are falling back. Now, I think, they are going to open their mortars along this side. So, I took my machine gun and crawled through the pipe to the other end and stuck it out there. I look, there the Germans come attacking. I put in a new magazine and emptied all of it. For, you know, the main thing in a war is to shoot, and where nobody cares. Take my word, I did not kill one single person in the war. I shot into the blue. But the officers see that you are trying, that the weapon emplacement is never still, and they think, 'That is good.'

"And so I got rid of the second and last magazine and stuck my head out again. There are no Germans. They are all leaving. Well, I think, now I'll go to Pan Boreisha and tell him that I have spent all my cartridges, that they must give me new ones, and, with that, I'll go have lunch.

"I crawl out and I don't believe my eyes. All the emplacements are empty. On the left and on the right. And there, where Under-Ensign Pan Boreisha used to be, rolls his hat with the white eagle, and a flask of whiskey. Pan Boreisha always drank when the shooting started.

"I don't get it. What's happening? Where are our Polish

battalions? I don't even see one dead body. Then I look back—and they come crawling. Our own troops. And Pan Boreisha without a hat. They go back to their emplacements and look at me as if I am from the other world.

"So what happened? Here's what. When the Germans attacked from the left side, they gave us the order to retreat. Pan Boreisha yelled to me, but I didn't hear because I had gone deaf before this and, on top of everything else, I was sitting in a pipe. Or maybe he didn't shout either. Anyway, both battalions retreated without me. And there I am thinking Pan Boreisha is keeping an eye on me, so I get rid of all my cartridges. The Germans decided not to throw themselves on a machine gun, so they withdrew and began an attack from the other side of the road. But by that time I had moved over there already, where I shot off all the rest of my cartridges. The Germans didn't take the chance and drew back to their initial positions. Our own troops, watching how it was going, came back to their emplacements and saw me.

"Laugh if you want to, but that's how it happened. Without knowing it, I held the defensive position all alone. Our headquarters declared that I was a hero and when it finally got to me that I had been left all alone in that pipe, I almost died from fright.

"Anyway, they made a big noise out of this. It was important for us to show the English what kind of lads we were, and the English command in Africa awarded me this important order, and even Pan Boreisha got a medal.

"It was from getting this order, I don't know what for, that all my misfortunes began. I was the only one in the whole detachment to bear the Cross of Victoria. And you think that made life any easier? Just the opposite. Our officers didn't like it at all that a Jew should have such a high order and they thought like this: so, Yan Lapidus bears the Cross of Victoria, well then, *proszę pana,* to the front lines with him, right into hell, to set an example for the rest of the men. Me. I had to set an example. Once again I say it. My conscience is clear. I never killed a single man. I wasn't less afraid than the others, but more. I only wanted to find my mama and I didn't want to die before then, very much.

"There were a lot of Poles in Africa. Some from Vilno even. But no matter who I asked, nobody knew anything about my mama.

"Then we landed in Italy. There they made 'commando' detachments. You know—crack troops? The first to go into battle and into the hottest places. Me, of course, the bearer of the Cross of Victoria, may it be damned three times, they shoved into the commandos. What I went through is impossible to retell. Have you ever heard of Monte Cassino? Mountains of Polish bones were left there to lie. I was there, too, and I don't understand how I got out alive. That's where these two orders from the Italian campaign come from. They gave them to all the survivors from the commandos, including me. For what? I don't know.

"There were also a lot of Poles in Italy. I searched for people from Vilno and asked about my mama. Nobody knew.

"They loaded us on troopships and carried us across the sea to England. There were even more Poles there. I met about twenty myself from Vilno. And not one who could tell me a thing about the fate of my poor mama.

"The Allies disembarked in Normandy. And who first? The commandos, of course. And who was in the commandos? John Lapidus. That's what they called me in England, John. For the liberation of France they gave the survivors the order of the Legion of Honor. This one here. The one and only decoration that helped me in life after the war. Otherwise, I would have starved to death.

"The war ended in '45. Everybody knows. But about Mama I knew nothing. They wouldn't let me into Russia where Vilno now was, because the Russians didn't like the Anders army.

"In 1939 I had gone East looking for Mama and now, after circling the whole globe nearly, I still had no results.

"After the war I became a nobody. They discharged me from the Army, but there was no trade for me. I began to drift around the world, to places where there were lots of Poles. There at least I could hope to find some kind of a trace. Where haven't I been? I've been in Brazil, working on the plantations. That was penal servitude. In Canada I was a lumberjack. And when I was down to my last penny and starving, the order of the Legion of Honor helped me. I enlisted in the Foreign Legion in France. That was fine company to find. All the outcasts of society. There were even some former members of the SS. Just imagine, I sleep side by side with one of them. There I ran into my Under-Ensign Pan Boreisha. He'd become a mercenary, too, because he'd run out of money and couldn't buy himself a drink. They called us the Black Legion and sent us to Indochina. The French were waging a war there with Ho Chi Minh.

"And what went on there? The horrors I saw! Before my very eyes Pan Boreisha killed two little children. Later God punished him for that. He fell into a 'wolf hole.' They were traps in the ground set with sharp spikes. The guerrillas made them and Pan Boreisha fell in. I saw what had happened, I heard his screams, but I didn't go help. Because he was a very bad man and deserved such an ugly death.

"For two years I suffered in Indochina. I got yellow fever and almost died. You can't drink the water there, it's nothing but bugs, and I don't like to drink whiskey. I couldn't get used to it.

"It will amaze you, but even in Indochina I met people from Vilno. One German from our Legion told me there was a very pretty Pole named Karolina in a whorehouse in Saigon and, apparently, she was from Vilno. So, *przepraszam*, I went to find this whorehouse and I put my money down and they brought me Karolina. I had never been in a whorehouse before and I never will be again. But that time I was. Karolina really had been born in Vilno, but she was there only as a child and couldn't tell me anything about my mama. All evening long we sang Polish songs together and we cried. And then we kissed like a brother and sister and I went away and left her all the money I had.

"Last year, finally, they let me back to Poland. I arrived a stranger to everyone and of no use to anybody. I didn't learn anything about Mama; then I began to petition the U.S.S.R. for a visa so that, after so many years, I could get to Vilno at last.

"And here I am. *Prosze pana*, lend me a cigarette if you can. I have started to smoke a lot and it gives me a cough. I don't have my health any more. A hundred years old, that's how I feel.

"Here in Vilno I found my mama. They informed me that she had been killed with other Jews as far back as 1942. This is official. But where she was buried nobody knows. Besides Panar, there are still two other communal graves. And who lies there is anybody's guess.

"I was at all three gravesites. By each one I sat and shed some tears. If it's not my mama who lies there, then other mamas do, and maybe there is no one to cry for them, because all the children are dead.

"Before I had hope at least. For fifteen years I was a searcher and maybe that kept me alive. I wanted to see my mama very much. What's left to live for now, *przepraszam*, I don't know."

Story of Jewish Parents,
Their Adopted Christian Daughter, Wanda,
and Their Late But Natural Son, Avremeleh,
As Told By Franya, the Cashier

Franya or Francheska, take your pick—like any good Catholic she had three names on her passport: Francheska Elzhbeta Felitsia—was hardly ever seen behind the partition labeled "Register," even though she was the cashier. She did literally everything here: boil the shaving water on the stove and carry it in steaming little glasses when the masters called for their "shaving set"; sweep up the different colored shocks of hair from the floor; wash the linen, clean and pick up the premises; run for cigarettes when they'd send her and, on top of all that, take the customers' money. The one thing she didn't do was draw up the records— she couldn't write. Yasha would do that. Besides his regular duties he was also the manager of the shop. A fact which Borukhovich considered a transparent injustice. Who was the experienced master here, anyway, Yasha or himself? Why, he'd had his very own establishment in Kovno once, with a telephone in it too, the only one on the street. Yasha: Who was he? Unlike Borukhovich, Yasha had learned to write a little Russian at the Front. That's why they'd appointed him even though he needed the position like a hole in the head. All it did was add to his headaches and since it was an extra office he only got half pay for it anyway. Money? It was enough to make you weep. He got twice as much in tips every day. But somebody had to be manager if there was going to be a barbershop, and Yasha was a soldier used to taking orders.

You weren't supposed to have a cleaning lady in the establishment. That you could do without. But a cashier? It was essential. Money needs managing and for that you had to have a responsible individual. Which Franya was, especially since she was a Christian—Polish or Lithuanian, it didn't matter. Around that time they were trying not to appoint Jews to positions of trust. They didn't inspire confidence. So, Franya was the cashier and the cleaning lady and, as they say, executive errand girl.

Franya: a resigned and harmless old maid with blotches on her cheeks and a head full of chronically uncombed hair, even though she did work in a barbershop. Her little potato of a nose was packed with adenoids. She had to breathe through her mouth and always kept it open. Which, of course, added nothing to her beauty. Every time she'd say something you'd want to make her blow her nose first. Then you could feel better.

As far as she could remember, Franya had always been an orphan. She'd been a maid of one sort or another all her life. That's why she spoke all the languages of the families she'd ever served, Polish and Lithuanian and Jewish, with such ease and so many mistakes. Actually she spoke them all at once and what you got was Russian salad. That was something they could all appreciate around here though, since they spoke the same, give or take a vegetable. Easy on the cabbage maybe, but heavy on the beets. No big difference.

Even though they didn't pay much attention to Franya on the whole, they were as used to her as to the green plush cloth edged with pompons that had covered the little round anteroom table since the dawn of time. If she'd gone out one fine day and never returned the place would have felt just as uncomfortable as if they'd suddenly taken the tablecloth and replaced it. Especially on Sundays when the widowers gathered.

They were all one big family. Even if they did tease her, they didn't offend Franya. Yasha and Borukhovich both regularly passed her a part of their tips to fill out her meager salary. Yasha more and Borukhovich less, not that it matters. Franya didn't need that much anyway. So what if she didn't have enough for shoes, she got along perfectly well in those high boots of Yasha's, his wife, Mirra, had brought her, and she wore them all year round. They were warm and dry. What more does a person need?

Franya loved to hear the stories they'd tell here in the barbershop. She'd respond straight from the heart, even cry a bit, and burst out laughing when they struck her as funny although, to tell you the truth, sometimes, she'd be the only one laughing.

"Give a listen, gentlemen, to what was in our town," she said from the partition reading "Register" on top. The conversation had died down and everybody was smoking reflectively.

They didn't ignore her, even though it was clear as day you couldn't expect anything interesting from her, or should you. This was a man's conversation. Call this a break. If a theater can have an intermission, then so can we. Besides, if a person wants to have his say, let him and be welcome. A chicken's no bird, as the saying goes, but Franya was a person too.

They all turned their eyes to the register and you didn't need a microscope to see they were looking at her the way a grownup looks at a child. The blotches on Franya's cheeks turned an even brighter red. Out of nervousness she started whipping up her light, undyed hangs of hair.

"Don't you look at me like that; it makes me red and I can't tell the story."

Everyone turned away submissively. Borukhovich described an incomprehensible arc with his razor over his customer's head and in one stroke swiped away the shaving cream from the temple to the chin. Which must have meant, "Go ahead and listen, but spare me if you don't mind."

"In our little town was a *mishpocheh*. A man and his wife. Her they called Noima and him, Sher."

"Franya, excuse me," Rabbi Arn stopped her. He was a gentleman and always treated everyone with respect, including Franya. "But for your information, Sher isn't a first name. It would have to be a family name."

"So who can make it out?" Franya brushed it aside, not too happy with the interruption. "A last name, then. That's what they called him anyway. Maybe because it was shorter and the first name was too long. That's what they went by, Noima and Sher. And God didn't give them children. Fifteen years they lived man and wife, but no matter what, no children."

"They couldn't have tried too hard," observed Yasha, still bending over his customer.

Franya was too embarrassed to go on. Borukhovich, though, didn't let the chance go by to take a dig at Yasha.

"A real *khultured* type," he said, without straightening up either.

"Jews, shame on you," said Rabbi Arn with mock sternness. "You're not giving the lady a chance."

At the word "lady," the blotches on Franya's cheeks caught fire and she gave Rabbi Arn a grateful look.

"They wanted their own child very much," she continued, "so they decided to take an orphan from the asylum. There were no Jew ones there so they agreed to a Christian child by the name of Wanda. Such a beautiful child this was that any would have taken her. Noima and Sher were crazy with her. They would dress her like a doll and Sher would order candies for her from Warsaw itself. She loved them like parents. Noima she called Mama and Sher, Daddy. This was the happiest *mish-*

pocheh in town. On a Saturday they would go out on the *gatva** and take turns holding her in their arms, first Noima, then Sher, and they would kiss her, and she would hug them with her arms and kiss them also. People would look at them, it was so *przyemne.*†

For some reason it grew very quiet.

Every face in the shop looked strained. Eyes saddened here and there and grew moist. They must have been remembering the children they'd had once, and held in their arms, and kissed. And where were those children now? Franya, Franya, you certainly picked a fine bunch to talk to about children.

But Franya didn't have the slightest idea of the feelings she was stirring up. Excited by her memories and pleased by the unexpected attention she was getting, she kept pouring salt on fresh wounds, as they say.

"Everything would have been all right, but when Wanda was ten, Noima—she didn't even dream of having her own child any more—suddenly she . . . well . . . you know . . ."

Franya, chaste maiden that she was, was ashamed to pronounce the word and Yasha came to the rescue.

"Got pregnant, right?"

Franya blushed and nodded. She didn't continue with her story, though. Rumpled Chloineh, the shoeshiner, unshaven and on crutches, took that moment to start knocking at the glass door from the street. He was trying to open it with his shoulder. Franya rushed out from behind the register and flung open the door in front of him. He tumbled into the barbershop on his one foot and without saying so much as a hello to anybody, started clattering with his crutches along the flagstones to the narrow door behind the register, trailing sharp, tarlike whiffs of

---

* *Gatva:* in Lithuanian, street.
† *Przyemne:* in Polish, nice.

the shoe cream he was steeped in through and through. By an unspoken agreement the barbers let Chloineh use their toilet. He worked on the street, after all, not in an establishment.

When the door to the toilet slammed shut everyone revived. Anytime Chloineh made an appearance they'd prick up their ears. From him you could expect anything.

"Nu, so what happened next?" someone asked impatiently.

Franya went back to her place behind the register, sat down, closed her eyes as if she were returning to the past that Chloineh's arrival had torn from her, and continued.

"There was born to them, to Noima and Sher, their own child, a *chłopchik.*‡ Avremeleh by name. Abramchik, that is. A child like any other. But it was their own and not from the asylum. Noima and Sher, they turned all their love to it and forgot about Wanda altogether. As if she had never been. Only Abramchik and Abramchik. Wanda they stopped dressing and forgot to feed. She went to sleep in the kitchen like a maid, and at nights she would have to rock Abramchik in the cradle when he cried. Wanda would go around such a mess that people in the town couldn't look at her, they felt so sorry. Other people called her into their homes and gave her something to eat and some kind of old clothes. But Noima and Sher didn't even want to look her way. They abused her from the bottom of their hearts and heaped all the work in the house on her."

"I'd have shot them like mad dogs!" wheezed Chloineh. He was standing in the doorway of the toilet, hanging on his crutches and buttoning up his fly. His little eyes blazed beneath his shaggy brows like coals; foam started bubbling in the caked and cracked corners of his mouth.

They all lowered their eyes and picked up their feet, letting him by. He clattered past on his crutches, dangling between

‡ *Chłopchik:* in Polish, boy.

59

them like a pendulum on his one and only leg. The door slammed behind him with a crash.

"Let God be their judge," said Franya and went on with her tale.

"Wanda became a nanny for Abramchik. She'd carry him and feed him and love him like nobody else on earth. She would show him to everybody and call him her own little brother. On account of this Abramchik her whole life had gone to pieces, you know, but she loved him so I cannot say how much.

"Now the Germans started taking all the Jews in the town to be shot. Noima and Sher they took, too, and Wanda grabbed Abramchik by the hand and ran beside with him into the column. Our own police were there from the town. They all knew that she was not a Jew, but from the asylum, a Christian child. Why should she die with the Jews? The police took her from the column themselves. Go, they said, hide, you are not a Jew. But her? She wouldn't. She clutched little Abramchik to herself and wouldn't leave Noima and Sher. So she went with them to the grave. And there she lies even now. With Abramchik, with Noima, and with Sher."

The customer got up from Borukhovich's chair. Freshly shaved and smelling of cologne, he passed by the hushed Jews to the register. Franya began to count his change out slowly, one bill at a time. She was trying not to give out too much, a mistake she'd made already more than once.

Story of the Count and the Jew,
As Told By the Count

The outside door flew open and a man entered the barbershop, his shaved head barely missing the lintel. There was something unusual about him, something captivating. Not that you could put your finger on it right away, but this one was different from the rest. Without bothering to hide their curiosity, they stared at him as he stood there by the door. And from a height unusual for someone so old, he looked right back with a kind of impersonal arrogance.

He was an odd mix. A proud, even dashing quality in a tall, dry, scrawny figure. And he wasn't a day under seventy. The face was something special, too. A mass of heavy wrinkles about the mouth and a nose, straight and strong, with nostrils that trembled as he breathed. And that downward gaze. It wasn't put on; with him, you could tell, it was a habit.

Even though it was bitter cold outside he came without a hat or coat. His clothes were in such sad shape you found yourself wanting to give him alms. The jacket was all soiled with dull splotches, old and worn before its time. The pants were bunched up at the knees and drooped on his thin buttocks from behind. They were so shredded at the bottom they lay like a fringe over his old soldier boots which, patched and tattered like the rest of him, still carried a fresh shine. The shirt had lost its color long ago and a carefully knotted tie lay on it, threadbare and crumpled, but still a tie.

"Who is the last in line?" Even his voice sounded out of the ordinary. Assured and strong, with that ounce of courtesy in it that's the dead giveaway of a well-bred person.

"Right this way, Count," smirked Yasha, winking to the rest of us and bowing and scraping before him with affected gallantry. "What is your wish?"

Franya burst out laughing behind the register, coughing so hard she started to choke. The others began to smile, shaking their heads and exchanging glances. That Yasha, what a sense of humor.

The tall old man turned his faded gray eyes on Yasha. The glance snuffed out the smile on Yasha's loose face and closed the thick lips over those gleaming metal teeth. Somehow Yasha didn't feel so good.

"That does great credit to your perspicacity," pronounced the old man with a barely noticeable smile. His bald head towered over the rest of them.

"Yes, I'm a count. A real one. Count Khadarkyavichus. Perhaps you've heard?"

The boots moved, the heels snapped, he strained his dry but still resilient frame and nodded briefly. Without bending his neck he bowed his bare skull.

"If you'll permit me, I'll sit. I am tired."

He sat down on the free seat, crossing his legs and mechanically hiking up his aged pants with the fringe, as if by habit. He had no socks. The boots had been drawn right over his bare feet with their blue bundles of veins. A large hole with diverging cracks gaped on the sole of his upper boot.

The Jews looked him over like little children. Yasha left his chair, leaned on the doorpost, and stared at him. Borukhovich, after shaving his customer, hustled about, consumed with curiosity. Now and then his bird beak pitched a look at the count.

Franya, her mouth packed full of something, stood stock-still, chewing.

The count sat up straight, gliding his empty gaze over their heads. All those intent looks left him completely cold. He was resting, his lids barely covering his eyes.

Everyone was silent. The only thing you could hear was Yasha's asthmatic wheeze.

The count put his hand to his jacket pocket and all eyes followed, as if they were still expecting a miracle to happen. All he took out, though, was a little cloth bag tied off with a string. An ordinary, old-fashioned tobacco pouch of the kind once popular during the war. He carefully got a folded piece of newspaper and tore off a section.

That's when the Jews began to move. Everyone reached for his own cigarettes and extended a pack to the count.

"My thanks," he refused the cigarettes, "I prefer shag. A Siberian habit."

He rolled a skillful cigarette, ran his tongue along the edge of the paper, and glued it shut.

The Jews started clicking their lighters and several fires danced in the count's face at once. He took a light, bowed his head in thanks, and with clear pleasure and satisfaction inhaled the sharp, stinking smoke. The barbershop filled with the stench.

"Unless I am mistaken you are all Jews," the count neither stated nor inquired, first taking us all in with a look that didn't stay on anyone too long. "I had assumed none were left after the war. I'm pleased to see I was mistaken."

Not knowing how to react to his words, the Jews began to nod anyway.

"What an irony of fate." The count smiled bitterly at his thoughts and wrapped himself up in a cloud of stinky smoke.

One of the Jews sighed. Just like that; out of sympathy. What the count had in mind by an "irony of fate," nobody knew.

"Before the war," said the count, not turning to anyone in particular—it was more like thinking out loud—"I didn't seek the company of Jews. My doors were closed to them. With one exception, it's true. The butcher was admitted, through the back door, of course, and only as far as the kitchen. This was, I believe, the only Jew to visit my home."

"What do you mean by that?" Yasha was on his guard.

"Nothing." The count didn't favor him with a glance. "Nothing. I merely state a fact."

And, smiling sadly, he continued.

"I was chief of the General Staff of the Lithuanian Army. Graduated from St. Cyr in France and the Academy of the General Staff in Berlin. And, prior to that, the law faculty of St. Petersburg University."

A look of respectful amazement crept over the faces of the Jews; Borukhovich, his razor hanging over the lathered face of a customer, stood perfectly still.

"All past," said the count, as if he were adding it all up, and the Jews nodded.

"It's been a month now since my return from Siberia. Alone, absolutely alone. Everything I own was on my back. No relatives, no friends. A total stranger. If anyone had recognized me, he wouldn't have offered his hand. No place for me even to spend the night."

Again the count took in the Jews with his faded gray eyes and gave a deep sigh.

"An irony of fate. The man I wouldn't let into my house any farther than the kitchen—I mean the Jewish butcher—recognized me on the street. Now, for the time being, I spend the night at his place. In the kitchen."

He drew a dry hand swollen with veins along his wrinkled face, shook his head as if to fight off some evil spell, and stood, carefully crushing his cigarette butt in the tray.

The Jews raised their knees to let him by. He went past, tall, thin, his chest out and his chin held high.

Borukhovich sprinkled a little cologne on his customer, tossed a cloth over his face, and rushed to meet the count with a honeyed smile, pushing Yasha out of the way.

"Count, I beg you."

And so Borukhovich shaved the count.

This you had to see. How he hopped and pranced about him, how he touched the count's big nose with the tips of his fingers, what childlike bliss brightened his face as he soaped the old man's cheeks. Borukhovich was on the peaks of ecstasy. For the first time in his long life as a barber he was shaving a count, a real count. An ex-count, actually, but a count all the same. His sickly self-respect, so trampled through the years, was having itself a holiday. This one moment was more than making up for a whole lifetime of suffering. The scant gray fluff on his flattened head trembled and gleamed. His round, birdlike eyes sparkled with a feverish glitter behind the thick lenses of his glasses. All the veins on his hooked nose popped through.

Not a minute would go by without his inquiring, "Count, does that trouble you? . . . Count, are you comfortable? . . . Count, some cologne?" stressing the word "Count" with special pleasure every time.

The count wasn't answering.

His straight, gristly nose with its trembling nostrils stuck out of the shaving cream, his heavy eyelids covered his eyes.

Fragrant beyond measure in a shower of cologne and sweeping clumps of hair on the floor with the fringe of his trousers, the count proceeded to the exit, trailed by a touched and mincing

Borukhovich. He stopped at the cash box, carelessly put his hand into his pocket, and tossed Franya a crumpled three-ruble note.

"But, Count, why?" groaned Borukhovich.

The count leveled a cold glance at him and finished him off with: "Keep the change."

Coming in line with the mirror, he smoothed out the tie on his chest. Then he opened the door, bowed good day to everyone, and lingering as if he were registering a complaint, said quietly:

"Cursed organism. It ought to die, but it won't."

With that he stepped on the top marble stair marked "Happiness."

The door closed slowly behind him with a dreary squeak.

Borukhovich broke the silence. "You've just seen a *khultured* human being." His eyes were still bright with bliss.

The Jews began to move around and smoke, expecting a pleasant discussion on all the fine details of the incident with the count. Borukhovich spoiled the fun. It's a good thing there weren't any new customers, because he wasn't going back to his seat. There he stood in the anteroom with the same feverish gleam behind his lenses that had already earned him the reputation of a not altogether normal human being.

By an unspoken agreement the group delicately avoided him and would patiently put up with his attempts to ruin their discussions. Borukhovich was a member of the family, too, just as much of a widower, just as lonely and without a place to perch. So what if he acted a little funny and tried to prove his superiority over them? He was quick tempered and he was absurd, but that was his misfortune, not his fault. Still, it was a wonder he hadn't gone crazy altogether and could manage a sensible conversation, even if it wasn't too intelligent. They got used to him. They put up with him and tried not to notice. And when he'd get troublesome they'd make up their minds to let it pass and yes him ironically.

This time Borukhovich had to have his say. The count had put him in a real state, and nobody was about to get in his way. Borukhovich held a razor he'd forgotten to leave on the table in his rush to see the count out the door. And now, as he waved it back and forth, it glinted unpleasantly, just like those bird eyes of his behind the lenses.

Story of a Cultured Human Being,
General Lelyushenko by Name,
and How He Esteemed His Very Own Barber,
Borukhovich, As Told By the Injured Party Himself

"You! The whole lot of you! Who do you think you are, anyway?" Borukhovich preached at the group in the high and mighty tones of the count. You could hear them in his voice, all right—a clear steal. "What contact have you ever had with *khultured* people? Manners! What do you know about manners! We just had a count with us, clear as day. And we enjoyed talking to each other. Why? Because we're both *khultured* human beings, that's why!"

There was another peculiar thing about Borukhovich. He had trouble speaking any of the languages used by the group: Yiddish, Russian, Lithuanian, or Polish. And to top it off, he completely swallowed and burred his *r*'s. He'd never given the world a sound even remotely like it.

"Now you listen to me." He crossed his arms on his chest and the tip of his razor bobbed dangerously close to his chin. "I'm going to tell you how one *khultured* individual meets another, and appreciates him, too. I stand here listening to you and it amazes me, simply amazes me. Jews, Jews, Jews, that's all you talk about. So what? I'm a Jew, too, but a *khultured* man besides, and that's why I get all the respect I'm due. So listen, just listen. Maybe you'll learn something.

"When the Red Army got to Osventsim I couldn't walk any more; I couldn't even lift a finger. A skeleton I was, all wrapped up in a blanket, laying naked by the crematorium. The Germans hadn't got around to burning me. They ran off too fast for that."

Borukhovich giggled, apparently remembering how the Germans had run. There was a senseless smirk on his face now, enough to make you feel a little nervous. He continued.

"The year before, my wife and two children had gone through the ovens. I survived, more like a corpse, though, than a living thing. To make a long story short, I was alive and thank God. I lay in a field hospital, recovered, got a little belly even, and started looking like a *khultured* individual again.

"Now, the commanding officer there, Lelyushenko, was a really *khultured* human being. The very most. He even demanded a private barber. So, they started looking. A master they needed, a real one, a *khultured* individual no less. And who do you think they got? Me, of course. They put me in a uniform. Even though I was a private they sewed it out of officer material, with a strap and waist belt. You know what kind of leather that was? Tops. Sometimes I'd even set my razor on it.

"I went to live with General Lelyushenko and was with him everywhere. Twice a day I'd shave him, morning and evening. Not just the beard, either, but the whole head. For a master like me that was child's play. In Kovno before the war I used to shape hairstyles for the artists and they didn't find anything to complain about. Here all I had to do was shave. The general was very pleased with me, and whenever I shaved him we'd talk. And he'd laugh a lot. Why? Because I'm nothing cheap, that's why, but a *khultured* human being, and I can be witty. People laugh, I tell you, and I like it.

"The general had an orderly. A man servant, almost, only in uniform. To shine shoes and sweep the floors. Vanya they called him. A simple country boy. As for *khulturedness*, not even a speck of it in him. He'd talk like a peasant and everybody would laugh at him.

"You want to hear how highly General Lelyushenko thought of me? Just listen. One evening some other generals and colonels were at his place to eat and drink. Even when he'd drink, Lelyushenko would remember his shave. A *khultured* human being. So, right in the middle of the spree he sends his orderly, Vanya, to come bring me. I take my instrument—a war trophy, it was, *Zollingen* Three Crowns—and together with Vanya I enter the hall where General Lelyushenko drinks with his guests.

"Vanya salutes and reports, 'Comrade General, the barber has arrived.'

"They all burst out laughing and I'll tell you why. Vanya was an ass, a simple country boy, and he couldn't pronounce the letter *r*. He didn't say 'barber,' but 'ballbeh,' with the letter *l*. Naturally they all died laughing."

Borukhovich began to titter himself, wiggling his bushy gray eyebrows over his horn-rimmed spectacles. In talking about Vanya, he'd pronounced "barber" without an *r* himself, replacing the sound with some kind of clank in the pit of his throat, never doubting that he'd said it right.

"So," Borukhovich continued laughing, "when they'd all had their laugh, General Lelyushenko says to me, 'Comrade Borukhovich,' he says, 'you are a *khultured* individual, teach Vanya how to say "barber."' Then they all cracked up. They knew it was easier teaching a bear to dance than getting Vanya to say 'barber' right. I laughed like all the rest. Then I told Vanya, 'Vanya, listen, it's so simple. All you have to do is speak slowly and draw it out.' And I show him: 'barrrrrrrber.'

"Well, the generals drop beneath the tables at that one. They could see Vanya wasn't going to make it. That's the truth, all right. 'Ballllllllbeh,' he says.

"Then I tell him, 'Vanya, relax. Just repeat after me, that's it, slowly, draw it out: 'barrrrrrrber.'

"How they laughed! And all of them at Vanya. A grownup and he can't pronounce his *r*'s. General Lelyushenko even turned red, he laughed so hard and I thought he was going to have a stroke. He calls me and he says, 'Thank you, Comrade Borukhovich. Continue in the same spirit.' And he shook my hand. That's the truth! And all the generals and colonels shook my hand. And they laughed so hard they couldn't stop. Poor Vanya. He really had them going with his pronunciation. And I laughed too. We were all *khultured* individuals and we understood each other. And Vanya, what was he? A simple bumpkin. Sure we laughed, what was the harm in that?"

No one in the barbershop was laughing, though, except for the storyteller. Borukhovich. Soft and little laughs, like a child's. They all looked at him sadly and felt uncomfortable.

"Hello, you vagabonds!" A deep, loud voice turned their heads. There was Mirra standing in the door. Yasha the barber's wife, a big woman (she'd gone stout long ago) with a massive chest that floated a little amber brooch on its side. Mirra was the only one in the shop with hair on her face: clear black mustaches and sideburns that dropped in ringlets below her ears. Threatening as she looked, though, she had a smile on her face as kind as her husband, Yasha's.

Mirra held a heavy bundle in either hand—a grocery bag bursting with paper packages and a whole collection of aluminum pans, fitted inside each other and attached to the same handle.

"Everybody here?" Moving her thick black eyebrows, Mirra looked the crowd over, and the crowd smiled back. This was an old friend, one of their own, who'd come each Sunday at this time with a clatter and a tasty fragrance from the pans.

71

"What smoke! You could hang a hammer from it." Mirra wrinkled up her nose. Nobody contradicted her either. Yes, they all nodded, they actually had smoked a lot, as a matter of fact, and you could hang a hammer from it, you might say, and the hammer wouldn't fall.

"Air out this establishment," ordered Mirra, and with a push of her foot she opened the door still wider.

"Well, what do you say, you vagabonds, getting hungry? Been at your wit's end, haven't you, waiting for Mama Mirra to come?" She gave a good-natured growl and made her way to the little table with her bundles. Everybody lifted his legs to let her pass.

"Plop. You've all landed in my lap. The whole lot of you. So, when are you going to get married already and have a family like everybody else and your own food on the table? I should live so long. The way things look I'll die first."

They smiled and nodded, accepting all her conclusions. Yasha hurried up with his last customer and took off his coat. Rabbi Arn scraped a few rubles together and sent Franya off for a small bottle of vodka. None of them drank, but there was a newcomer after all, and things ought to be done up right.

"Wash your hands. March!" Mirra ordered loudly, setting the dishes on the table. Everybody lined up obediently to wash his hands at the faucet.

"Looks like there's a spoon missing." Mirra scratched her sideburns. "What am I saying? There's enough and still left over. I'm always ready for surprises. And Chloineh, why haven't they called him yet? Where is that *shlimazl?*"

She stuck her head out the door and shouted to the shoeshiner. Loud and for the whole street to hear.

"Chloineh! You need a special invitation? Come eat before

they gobble it all down. And get a newspaper to spread on the table."

And Chloineh, the nervous wreck, Chloineh, the quick-tempered, obeys like a model child. He puts his brushes back in the box, fastens the padlock, jumps up on his one leg, and, holding the wall with his hand, neatly takes *Soviet Lithuania* down from its stand, with those caricatured long noses so like his own, and the articles about the assassins in the white lab coats, and the topical satire on the Jew spy from Vilno. He folds the paper, sticks it into his pocket, snatches up his crutches, and swinging like a pendulum, jumps up the three marble steps. *Droga* on the first one, *do* on the second, and *Szczes'cia* on the third. Up he goes into the barbershop, pointing the way to happiness and clattering on his sticks.

For the last time Mirra stands in the doorway and turns a little metal tablet on a string to the other side. Instead of the word "Open," passersby can now read "Closed for Lunch."

You know, when I think of Vilno now those three steps come suddenly to mind. White marble they were, with a Polish word etched into each one in red granite:

DROGA

DO

SZCZĘS'CIA

As if there were no other historical sights.

Not long ago I went back for the last time. There were some passengers in my compartment who'd never been to Vilno before. Thoroughly polite and cultured human beings, as Boru-khovich, the barber, would have put it. I told them about the town. About the three marble steps, about The Road to Happiness barbershop, about the people who'd gather there on a Sun-

73

day because they didn't have to work, and there was nowhere else for a lonely person to go, and about the stories that I heard.

This you won't believe, but my companions got so involved they asked me to take them straight from the train station to the corner of Gedimin and Tatarsky and show them the barbershop and its three steps. They even agreed to pay for the cab themselves.

I took them. On the way I felt strangely excited, as if I were about to show them not just a barbershop and three steps, but something very near to my heart.

Well, I wasn't excited in vain. Apparently the feeling had been some kind of premonition. Gedimin and Tatarsky were there all right, but the barbershop wasn't. The entire bottom floor had been rebuilt long ago; an office of some sort was there now. To get to the main point, though, the three steps had disappeared. White marble they were, with a Polish word etched into each in red granite:

DROGA

DO

SZCZĘS'CIA

The entrance was somewhere else entirely. Sinister gray steps of cement lay there now instead. God knows where the marble ones had gone.

I found myself in a very unpleasant position. It was beginning to look like I'd told a pack of lies. And how was I going to vindicate myself? If someone had shown me where those steps had gone, I'd have given him plenty. They'd have been my witnesses, those steps.

But who could find them now? Later I walked the streets of Vilno, hoping to find at least one familiar face. A totally useless undertaking, it turned out. In such a large city, after so many years.

And if I had found someone still alive, Rabbi Arn, Yasha, the barber, Chloineh, the one-legged shoeshiner, even, would they have corroborated it? I ask you. They'd have shrugged their shoulders and looked at me like a not altogether normal human being. "Why the big fuss? Some people sat in a barber-shop and for nothing better to do they shot the breeze. That's all. So what's to corroborate?"

And, you know, I think they'd have a point.

Legends
from Invalid Street

From the Author

It's no secret: Jews don't roll their r's. Not on your life. Call it one of our national characteristics. Anti-Semites can spot us right off with it. Russian has a hard r, you see, and we don't. What are you going to do?

The only people in our town to roll their r's were the authorities—all of whom were Russians—and the woodcutters—people who'd go from house to house with saws and axes getting odd jobs chopping wood. They were Slavic, too.

The rest of the population got along perfectly well without so much as a ripple in their r's.

On the revolutionary holidays, the first of May and November the seventh, when large demonstrations were organized in our town like everywhere else, the Russian authorities would stand in the rostrum and greet the marching columns with a hearty cry. "Long Live the Builders of Communism!" they'd holler, and we'd all answer with a loud "Hurrah!" And there's not an ear alive that could have caught a single r rolled in our cry.

That was the town where I was born.

It had a street called Invalid. Friedrich Engels Street they call it now, after the founder of scientific Marxism, and to hear it you'd think he'd been born there instead of me.

Still, when I think back to that street and the people who

once lived there, may they rest in peace, it remains Invalid Street in my mind.

That's why I've called the stories I plan to tell you, "Legends from Invalid Street."

My Uncle/Legend Number One

They called my uncle, Simcha.

Simcha. In Hebrew it means joy, happiness, a festive occasion. Whatever you like, as long as it wouldn't bear the slightest resemblance to him.

Maybe he was born laughing, and that's how he got the name. If that's the truth, his first laugh was also the last. Nobody, including me or anyone who knew him before I was born, ever saw Simcha laugh. Not once. This was a man, may he rest in peace, dismal and sad as they come. But quiet, and good.

And the last name, Kavalerchik, "the little cavalier," just like the first one, out of the blue. Not Kavaler or, if worst came to worst, Kavalerovich, but Kavaler*chik*. Why so fancy?

He was no dandy, not by a long shot. All the time I knew him he wore the same old suit, its colors bleached to nothing in the sun, the material darned and patched here and there by my aunt Sarah. He always looked the same: ordinary. God forbid he should ever smell of cologne.

Maybe back in Czarist times his grandfather or great-grandfather had a local reputation as a dandy, and since the family line was frail and undersized, the village policeman couldn't think of anything better when he got around to naming the Jews than Kavalerchik, "the little cavalier."

Anyway, that's what they called him. Simcha Kavalerchik. Take it or leave it, that's your business, but God help you to spend your life the way Simcha Kavalerchik did.

There were no weaklings on our street. The other streets knew what they were talking about when they called our people *aksonim,* studs if you want the literal meaning. Mythic giants, to be poetic.

When you think about it, though, how could we be weak? One whiff of our air would make a stallion out of a chickadee.

As far back as I can remember, our street always smelled of hay and dill. Everybody kept cows and horses in their yards; the dill grew in the kitchen gardens and wild along the fences. Those two smells didn't even leave us for the winter. Every day they'd bring the hay in on sleighs, and the snow on all the streets and sidewalks would be strewn with smelly armfuls of the stuff. And the dill? Every winter they'd open up the barrels of pickled cucumbers and tomatoes in the cellars and at least half of them were dill. Such a smell would roam the streets it would make your head spin and your knees go a little weak if you weren't used to it.

Most of the men on the street were *balagulas.* Draymen and wagoners, that is. The breed's extinct now, like the mammoths. One of these days, when archeologists start excavating the communal graves laid down by World War Two, somewhere on the Volga or the Dnieper or even the Oder in Germany, among your run-of-the-mill human bones they're going to find backbones and shinbones big as a behemoth's. Just so they don't waste their time with Latin nicknames and whistling in the dark, I'll give them a hand right now: Gentlemen, you've stumbled on the remains of a *balagula* that once lived on our street before the war, that's all.

The *balagulas* kept their own horses and they were special, too. Strong and sound Russian cart horses with massive, shaggy legs, necks like bulls, and hindquarters so broad five of us kids could sit on one of them at once. But these *balagulas* were no cowboys. They didn't go riding around on those horses; no sir, they took pity. The flatcars those beasts dragged carried up to five tons. How could you think of riding them after that?

In the winter when it was slippery and a *balagula* led his horse to drink, he'd be ready to carry the thing on his shoulders right to the pump. No horseback rider here.

A *balagula* was no cowboy, all right, but he could make mince-meat out of whole posses if he wanted. When they started giving Jews a break after the Revolution and offering them a crack at the leading jobs, a number of *balagulas* just couldn't resist the temptation and became coaches in some of the more demanding sports. They'd break records like sunflower seeds. The wrestling champion of the Black Sea Fleet, Yan Strizhak, was from our town and his father, Chaim Katznelson, the *balagula*, lived right on our street. Disapproved of his son, too. Maybe that's why Yan Strizhak never came to visit.

So, assuming you believe even one word of what I've been saying, you may want to ask how there could have been such a weakling on our street as my uncle, Simcha Kavalerchik.

For that I've got an answer. In the first place, Simcha Kavaler-chik wasn't born on our street or even in our town, but some-where else. Besides, if you want to call a spade a spade, he wasn't even my uncle. Not until he married my aunt Sarah, anyway. And at seventy Aunt Sarah could still carry a hundred double-bucket loads from the well to water the garden and chop the firewood herself, let the same be said of all good Jews.

It looks like we've gotten off the track. I wanted to tell you about my uncle, Simcha Kavalerchik, a story that has nothing to do with physical strength. It's the soul of a man I want to deal with.

As one great writer put it, the eyes are the mirror of the soul. Simcha's eyes, like the rest of him, were small, but so good and honest I can see them now. The very eyes, I'm sure, that won Aunt Sarah's heart.

Right after the Revolution this was. The Civil War was going on and our town, as they say, was busy trading hands. First the Whites would take it, then the Reds, then the Greens, then the Germans, then the Poles. There weren't any pogroms, it's true. I'd like to see you try touching a Jew from our street. Kaput, that's it, you could count the war lost right there and then. Nothing would help you either, heavy artillery or machine guns included.

Back then, my aunt Riva told me, when she was still a very pretty girl, a Polish officer once saw her home from a dance. Spurs on his feet, a saber at his side, a four-cornered Confederate cap with a white eagle on his head, winding white aglets on his chest. The works. A doll this was, not an officer. Anyway, he lingered a little too long at our gate. Not that he made advances, nothing that stupid. He just wanted to prolong the joy of being with Aunt Riva a little bit. But to my uncle Jacob, her brother, this was already too much. He took a shovelful of fresh manure and smacked it right through the fence, all over the officer's head. Right on the cap and right on the aglets.

The Poles are a proud people, everybody knows. And a Polish officer is even prouder. This one snatched his saber right out of the scabbard, and got ready to hack Uncle Jacob to pieces. Especially since Jacob wasn't even fully of age; he'd just turned thirteen. So what do you think happened? Like child's play, Aunt Riva yanked the saber out of the officer's hand and let him have it, only flatwise, of course, right in the rear. He darted down the length of the street, dropping cow plop from his hat and shoulder straps, and no one ever saw him round there again.

The saber lay in our garret and I used to play war with it. There were Latin letters written on the hilt, and when we started studying foreign languages, I learned what they said. It was the owner's name, Pan Borowski. If he's still alive somewhere, this Pan Borowski, he can back me up, firsthand.

So, the Civil War was raging and Simcha Kavalerchik was about eighteen.

Sickly, narrow-shouldered, with a sunken chest, he'd sit for days on end bent over a joiner's bench in his boss's cellar shoe-shop, watching the world go by through a narrow little window under the ceiling. A world of feet and footwear; from his angle there was nothing else to see. He'd watch the broken boots of the Reds, all bound up with bits of rope, he'd watch the bast shoes of the peasants and the stolen patent leather of the Greens, he'd watch the heavy-shod boots of the Germans and the stiff, bottle-shaped boots of the Poles, all spruced up and ready for review.

There it was, flashing by and catching his eye whenever he'd take it off his work for a second. Then he'd go back to his hammer and pound new soles into the old leather of the townspeople, brought to rags and tatters by the war.

I've said it already: He was weak and he was quiet, he didn't know how to read or write, and he wasn't interested in politics. Making ends meet was all he tried for and, once in a blue moon, showing up on the street. There was nothing but uncertainty and terror out there. Anyone who wanted to could beat him to a pulp. The way he saw it, they were all stronger and almost all of them bloodthirsty.

That's probably how he'd have stayed too, for the rest of his life. But one day, lifting his bloodshot eyes from the bench, he saw a pair of boots in the window so sensational they set his mind on fire. Curiosity: Name me a Jew that suffers from

85

a lack of that. Simcha was no exception. One look at those boots and he was a slain man. He had never seen anything like them before. Dusty, box calf boots, the tops dashingly turned back on the sides, and officer's cockades fastened here and there all along the leather like a collection of trophies. Shoes, hell, this was an art show!

His boss—a stingy man, a mean man, the man Simcha feared more than anyone else on earth—had just come back in from the street. In a voice quivering with fear, looking around and whispering prayers, he told his apprentices exactly who those other worldly boots belonged to.

The Twenty-fifth Chongarsky Division of Budenny's First Red Cavalry, the fiercest of the Reds, had just come into town. The very men who'd knock a White officer's head off in battle, rip the cockade from his cap, and fasten it to the side of their boots. To keep a running count of enemy dead. What's more, the boss said, they'd just ordered the whole town to gather for a meeting in the square. As for him, he wasn't going, no, he wasn't that stupid, and his advice to the others, if they wanted to keep their heads on their shoulders, was the same.

Simcha hated his boss so much and was so ready to do something to spite him that he just upped and disagreed. For the first time ever he openly disobeyed him and that first time was fatal. He climbed out of the cellar and into the light of day, let the fresh air into his sunken chest, and, not a little scared, looked around.

The streets were full of music, accordions playing, all kinds of uproar. The unimaginable was happening. Red cavalrymen, with their high cheekbones and slanting highwayman's eyes, their forelocks popping out of their sheepskin hats, were dancing with the Jewish girls who, for all their blushing and mincing, weren't the slightest bit afraid. This was a first. It looked as if

86

the rich had just been blown away. The poor had taken over the streets—there they were, rejoicing with the cavalrymen, shouting with all their might. This was another first for Simcha, too.

Life was changing. Something new and unknown had come in off the wind.

"Hey! Everybody's equal! No more rich and no more poor! Jews and Russians, simple workingmen, one class, one united family! Up with the shacks, down with the palaces!"

Simcha heard those passionate, hoarse speeches at the meeting, his head spun, and he believed. He wanted to a lot. He believed, with a fire in his breast and forever, with all the passion of a pure and simple heart, pining for justice and a fair deal.

He wasn't going back to the boss in the basement any more.

When the squadrons of the Twenty-fifth Chongarsky Division left town, among those dashing troopers prancing lightly on their breakneck steeds, trotting off in clouds of dust for the Front, people saw a pitiful sight, barely hanging on to its horse. Simcha Kavalerchik it was. A Jewish boy, sickly and frail, scared of everything on earth, people and horses both. Like a sleepwalker, he'd volunteered for Budenny, and no one had chased him away, no one had even made fun of him.

They called him Comrade, they hung a heavy sword on him, they set the furry *papakha* back on his head as it started to slip down over his eyes, and for the first time in his life he clambered up a horse's back. In the saddle he started to shake and rock, he couldn't reach the stirrups with his feet, he clutched the reins convulsively, and in clouds of dust, with lots of whooping and whistling, he disappeared, lost in a horsy avalanche that roared straight toward the unknown and maybe even death.

He didn't die, though. Not my uncle. Otherwise, there'd be nothing left to tell you. When the Civil War was just a dying rumble, he came back to town. It was like coming out of no-where; everybody had forgotten all about him.

How he pulled through and in one piece God only knows. He was a rotten storyteller. Squeezing something sensible from him was out of the question. Besides, he'd lost most of his voice in the war and what was left was hoarse, hard to hear, and even harder to make out. As far as I could understand it from him, he'd wrecked his voice during his first cavalry attack. Swinging his sword and blind to everything, he'd rushed ahead at a full clip with the rest of them. All his strength had gone into staying on his horse. He was crazy with fear and pitched out this wild, heartrending, savage shriek, just like everyone else. He must have screamed louder than the rest, though, since he damaged his vocal cords for life. For a long time after he couldn't even talk, and to the day he died he never could do more than squeak whenever he wanted to say something.

The war hadn't made him a bit stronger. He was the same, puny and frail, and, on top of everything else, as bowlegged as any other horseman. Those wide leather riding breeches he'd worn back home made his legs look like a regular wheel. Along with the calluses his poor horsemanship had packed like rocks into his skinny butt, he brought back scores of Russian words from the Front, including obscenities and out-of-the-way expressions like "communism," "Marxism," and "expropriation." He stopped using the first bunch right away. He was a gentle man and didn't mean to hurt a soul. To make up for it, he used the second bunch as often as he could and usually in the wrong places. Such a feverish gleam would come into his eyes, though, that you just decided not to argue the point.

He came back to town a hundred per cent Bolshevik with a belief in communism like no rabbi ever had in his Torah. Nothing else on earth existed for him. He was ready to give up eating, drinking, and sleeping if necessary to keep communism healthy and rosy-cheeked. No mother ever loved her child the way he loved his idea. He'd have eaten anyone alive that stood in its path, even though, and I'll say it again, he wasn't a bloodthirsty person, but good and fair. So honest it made you sick. The first to suffer for it were his family, my poor aunt Sarah, that is. God knows why she married him. Maybe it was the riding pants, maybe just the general shortage of husbands after the war and her fear of ending up an old maid. I won't even exclude the possibility of a little ulterior motive. After all, the Bolsheviks were in charge in Russia and Simcha was a pure-blooded Bolshevik with such a record that Aunt Sarah must have expected, once she was his wife, to make her way in the world and be nearer the pie when the victors got around to slicing it up.

I don't know. I'm just supposing. Aunt Sarah was a child of such dire poverty we should never know again; it was only natural she'd like a little light to burn in her window, too. And Simcha Kavalerchik, the Bolshevik, stood a better chance of getting it going than anyone else. The new power was his power. He was the power himself.

A peaceful life was starting up for everyone. Socialism, the building of "the first phase," was under way. People were coming back to life, stretching and stirring, putting their noses to the breeze and getting the hang of things.

We had a street full of enterprising people. No matter how hard the New Order pressed them for taxes, nothing happened. After all, even if the revenue inspector wasn't from our street, he was a person too. Give him a little and he'd overlook a lot. You know the saying: If you don't grease a wheel it won't go? Well, there's a pile of sense to that. Sometimes, to squeak by, you have to go sideways, and people were squeaking by. Even getting rich. And building new homes and buying furniture.

The wide necks of the *balagulas* were getting ruddier and ruddier, and their wives' bottoms so big their enemies just about popped with jealousy.

Simcha Kavalerchik didn't build himself a new home or buy himself new furniture. How could he? He was the only man on the street not to bilk his Soviet state. He lived off his salary alone. Period. And yet, there he was, holding a position beyond the wildest dreams of Invalid Street. He'd become the assistant director of the Meat Packing Plant, the first milestone of socialism in our town and for a long time our only large-scale industrial enterprise. Simcha kept that post for the rest of his life, right up to the Second World War and after. Mr. Assistant Director.

They'd have been happy to make him director, too, but to the end of his days he never learned how to read or write very well. As for lowering his post or firing him, even that would have been blasphemy, a spit in the face of the whole Bolshevik Party. Because there was no Bolshevik in the whole town like Simcha Kavalerchik and, from the look of things, won't ever be again. Besides, he wasn't just a Bolshevik, he was a very honest man, and work meant everything to him.

You want the understatement of the age? Simcha loved his Meat Packing Plant more than a wife and child. If I said that outside of it nothing even existed for him, I wouldn't be wrong. Nothing except the lot of the workers in the "countries of capital," maybe, which he took to heart, and the world revolution, which he expected impatiently from day to day and never gave up hoping for.

The Meat Plant, to use a term from the papers, was his "favorite child." Even though Simcha was management, and management, as everybody knows, is supposed to sit in an office behind a desk, nobody ever saw him there. He'd do whatever job came to hand like a regular worker. He'd dig holes, he'd set posts, he'd lay bricks and raise the walls, and when they installed the massive machines with a "heave ho!" in the shop, he'd be there with the rest, propping them up with his skinny shoulders, his heart in his mouth at the very thought that one careless move might break even the tiniest screw—these were machines from overseas, after all, bought with gold, and a kopeck of the state was dearer to Simcha than one of his own.

As a matter of fact, Simcha didn't have a kopeck of his own to claim. What did they pay him, anyway, but tears? Not that he ever thought about it. Only work, only building communism, just a little faster.

Back then the plant still didn't have a dining hall. During the lunch break the workers would take out the food they'd brought from home and eat it right in the shop. They'd munch into chicken legs, wash them down with bottles of milk, and with a kind of lazy politeness listen to my uncle make speeches. He didn't eat during the lunch break. What could he bring from home, anyway, but the hole from a bagel and the cuffs off a vest? On an empty, sunken, rumbling stomach, Simcha would spend the lunch break on agitation and propaganda. From all the fiery speeches he'd heard in Budenny's First Cavalry he adapted a little something of his own, and for the rest of his life and every lunch break, a hungry man, he'd tell the chewing crowds in words that were hoarse and voiceless, but full of fire, about the bright future that awaited them under communism when all would know abundance and all would brothers be.

And these builders of communism, in their country shoes and *balagula* homespun coats, would sit there sinking their strong teeth into their privately owned suet and chicken legs, drinking their privately owned milk straight from the bottle with a gurgle, and, take it or leave it, they'd believe him. Not what he said, but what he was, Simcha Kavalerchik. How could you not believe in his honesty?

My aunt Sarah, the only one of her sisters, you'd think, to make a good match by marrying a Bolshevik, was the most unhappy woman on earth. That's what Mama said. And all of Invalid Street said the same.

Judge for yourself. All around you people are building their own homes, buying furniture, living like human beings, and wishing the Revolution long years of life. Under the Czar when everything was private there was little to pilfer and nothing to appropriate and now, with the coming of freedom, you could take a little, filch, and snatch as long as you weren't a *shlimazl* and didn't get caught. And Aunt Sarah? Not only didn't she build her own home, she didn't even get an apartment in the multistoried Home of the Commune, where all the Bolshevik families, exclusive, had moved. Her husband, Simcha Kavalerchik, had absolutely refused to write an application for an apartment there. He'd die of shame first, he told Aunt Sarah. The country was still full of homeless people; when everyone else had a roof over his head, *then* he'd agree to take an apartment, but not before. Otherwise, as my uncle explained it to his silly wife, why make a Revolution in the first place and stir up such a mess?

So they took a room in someone else's house on our street and paid rent straight from my uncle's bare salary. After that what was there left to live on? I told you already, tears. But Simcha Kavalerchik didn't grieve. He even had children, two of them. A son and a daughter, my cousins. And at the insistence of their father, the Communist, they were given such a pair of names that all Invalid Street could do was shrug its shoulders for a long time to come. The boy they called Marlen and the girl, Jeanna. In honor of the Revolution. Marlen: the union and abridgment of the names of the two captains of the world proletariat, Marx and Lenin. Marlen. And Jeanna, in honor of the French Communist Jeanna Laburbe, leader of an armed uprising of French sailors in Odessa during the Civil War.

Somehow, Jeanna and Marlen had to be fed and clothed. Simcha didn't think about that, though. Not because he was a bad father; he just didn't have the time.

Socialism was entering a new phase. Collectivization had begun. In other words, they were collecting all the cattle and all the land of the peasants into common property so they could put an end to exploitation and let everyone lead an equally happy life. Only, the peasants didn't get the point and held on to the land by the skin of their teeth. What couldn't be taken clean had to be taken anyway. And so, all over the countryside, the land came up with blood.

The Communists would shoot the stubborn, disobedient landowners who refused to live the happy life of the kolkhoz and, to get even, the peasants would shoot the Communists in the back, slaughter them in their sleep, and chop them up with axes. No denying it, everyone had a ball.

They'd send Communists from the towns into the struggle with the politically unconscious peasantry. There was only one Communist on our street, Simcha Kavalerchik, one of the very first to come thundering down for collectivization. No one had to push him; it was voluntary. Happiness was all Simcha Kavalerchik wanted for the peasants, from the very bottom of his heart. And so, armed with a pistol, he set out for the sticks, to talk the peasants into entering the kolkhozes and being happy once and for all.

Barely pronouncing the Russian words, voiceless and hoarse, with a heavy Jewish accent, he walked straight into hell, right to a village where every Communist before him had been hacked to eternity. Swinging his pistol, he went from hut to hut and drove the people to a meeting. There, in a smoke-filled, over-crowded hut, he made his fiery Bolshevik speeches.

Try picturing it for a minute.

A village hut. The walls ribbed with logs. Thick beams hanging heavy from a low ceiling. Little windows frosted through and through. Outside there's a blizzard howling and the woods moan for miles.

The hut. Crowded with men and women, sitting in their sheepskin coats smoking their shag and pitching dirty looks from under their woolly caps at the frail, little character with the Jewish nose. There he is, flitting before them in the corner beneath the icon of St. Nicholas the Intercessor, while the dim lamplight casts his trembling shadow back into their sweaty faces, flushed with heat and anger.

Here in the backwoods, since Czarist times, they've given Jews no credit for being human, and Communists they hate with a vengeance. Now they have to put up with incoherent, un-Russian speeches from a man who's both.

The women sink beneath my uncle's hoarse, confusing words, they look into his fiery eyes as he draws them pictures of their happy lives in the kolkhoz, if only they'll listen to him, Simcha Kavalerchik, and do everything the Party instructions say, and from the bottom of their hearts they cry and cry. How long already have they known what lies in wait for this God's fool, this mad and righteous man? He'll leave the hut in an hour or two, go out in the cold, and then what? An ax in the back. Or a stake to open his head. He won't have been the first. But those others, they were built like men at least, not like this one, this twig you could, forgive the expression, snap with your snot.

A pretty little picture, don't you think? Enough to make your skin crawl. And what about him? Wasn't he afraid? I'll tell you:

No. Spit in my eyes three times if you want, but it's the truth. If he had been, he'd never have made it out of there alive. It wouldn't have been an ax that killed him either, but fear itself.

He was afraid of nothing because he thought of nothing but this: He was a Communist with an assignment to complete for the Party. At any price. His own life, even, if that's what it cost. What was it worth to him if the Revolution needed it? Do you understand now? He just didn't have the time to think about himself.

All month long, not a word from him. For a whole month he lives in a den of wolves. He sleeps in those huts right beneath the icons and dreams a Communist's dreams. Dreams of Ilyitch's little lamps* burning from the smoky ceilings, tractors humming in the fields, and happy peasants living free of grief, holding hands and dancing through the woods.

Meanwhile, the blizzard rages all around him, the forests moan, and an ax with his name on it flashes in the light.

It's hard to believe, but he came back alive. In fact, they even established a kolkhoz in the village, and the only reason they didn't name it after Simcha Kavalerchik, I figure, was that it didn't sound right for a kolkhoz somehow. They named it after Stalin, and the men my uncle pleaded with and persuaded from the bottom of his heart are still there waiting for their lives to turn happy.

In time some of his promises did come true. Ilyitch's little lamps began to glow, tractors started droning in the fields, and the people of the kolkhoz even had their dances in a ring, whenever management wanted. But That-Happiness-Such-As-There-Never-Was still wasn't. Let's not blame my uncle, though. There's nothing he wanted more than to make them

---

* The term then used for electric bulbs.

happy. It just so happened that even Karl Marx, who was God to my uncle, couldn't see everything coming.

He returned and was wheezing out speeches at the Meat Plant the very next day as if nothing had ever happened. The years passed, the kids grew up, and Aunt Sarah lived worse than anyone else. We'd lend her money and never ask for it back. Everyone felt sorry for her and the children, looked on Simcha Kavalerchik as a lost cause, and waited to see how it would all turn out.

All those years he wore the same old clothes he'd come back in from the Civil War. The boots had been patched up a hundred times, the trousers and tunic were patch piles, too. But Simcha wasn't sorry. What about? He didn't even notice how he was dressed. In fact, he'd have gone around in the same things for another twenty years if the Second World War hadn't come along and they'd called him up. The Army issued him the standard uniform, and at long last he parted with his rags and started looking decent.

He left for the Front, and for four years while the war lasted didn't know where his family was or what had happened to it. He knew the Germans were killing all the Jews they could get their hands on, and since our town had been occupied, he naturally assumed that neither his wife nor his children had survived. You could never say he wasn't sorry. He was a husband and a father and, I've said it, a good man on the whole. But his whole being was troubled by thoughts of a higher order. There was no way he was going to let the Soviet Union lose the war or see the work of the Revolution perish. Where was there time to mourn a family?

When the war ended, Simcha Kavalerchik was a major in Berlin. He'd been a political worker in the Army. Rather than hang out in the rear, he'd joined the advancing troops in the hottest places and gone into the attack with the infantry like a common soldier, forgetting that he was a major and that it was his duty to stick a little closer to headquarters. I think the soldiers loved him. In spite of the fact that reading and writing weren't his strong points and maybe just because, in spite of that heavy Jewish accent and hoarse whisper of a voice, they had a certain sympathy for him, compassion even. Besides, that completely unmilitary figure of his, those ungainly, broad shoulder straps on those skinny, sloping shoulders, that absolutely unselfish concern for others and never for himself, all showed him to an advantage over the other officers and won him the soldiers' hearts.

He came back alive and well in a new officer's uniform of fine English cloth with more medals on his chest than he had room for. Those little bronze circles bumped right into each other. The very first thing he did was take them all off, and no one ever saw them again. Out of modesty he did it. There was nothing in medals to be proud of, he told me later, and no reason to show them off. He'd come back alive but others hadn't, and what could his medals do but make widows weep?

He found his family in one piece. At first he was very surprised and then happy, of course.

There was a sharp housing crisis after the war, and once again they went to live with others.

The war hadn't sobered my uncle up one bit. He raised the Meat Packing Plant from its ruins and became its assistant director again.

Even though we never saw it in the stores, the plant produced a first-rate, high-quality dry sausage. It was all exported. And Simcha, the head of the whole operation, never once brought even a link of that sausage home. Later he confessed to me he'd tried it once, when he'd been appointed a member of the tasting board.

Little by little, life in town returned to normal. People built houses, bought furniture, and snatched at whatever came their way. Only my uncle, Simcha Kavalerchik, could be satisfied on a diet of pure ideas.

Meanwhile stealing was flourishing at the plant. In their shirts, in their pants, under their hats, workers were walking off with links of sausage, giblets, pieces of meat. An armed guard was posted at the main gate to search everyone who left the plant. They'd catch the thieves, widows and war casualties mostly, prosecute them, and ship them off to Siberia. Nothing helped. Meat and sausages kept on disappearing. Later they discovered the guards were stealing, too.

Simcha Kavalerchik's head took a spin, and the ground beneath him slipped away. Forever hungry, lean and dry, he'd step up at the meetings and make threats and demands and plead with the people not to betray themselves, their humanity. Be honest. Don't steal. Just a bit more and we'll have communism built, and then all our problems will fall away and there'll be enough for everyone. They'd all thank him then, all these people, for stopping them in time.

Nothing helped.

The state was building factories and plants. Fresher sources of funds were desperately needed, and every year the state would announce a new loan the workers had to give up a month's pay for, just like that. The workers didn't want to, of course. My uncle, to set an example, laid out three months' pay in advance.

His family was simply starving to death. Aunt Sarah had already lost all hope. People all around her were getting by somehow, and she didn't know one bright day. The children were growing up, and there was no way, no way at all, to feed or clothe them. Simcha himself had worn out his Front-line uniform of English cloth. And Aunt Sarah, like a virtuoso, kept laying new patches on old to keep it from turning into a rag. My uncle couldn't have cared less.

He'd come home in the evening from work, take a seat by the window in their tiny little room and open the newspaper. Meanwhile, his wife, her back turned to him would grumble and warm up some kind of broth on the stove.

As he'd read the paper his dry, exhausted face would let go of some of its wrinkles and begin to shine. The papers would write of new workers' victories and the blooming of the land. At times like that he'd get the feeling everything was going perfectly— just a few unrelated problems and those only in the town where he lived.

"Sarah," he'd turn to his wife, his hoarse voice suddenly tender, "Sarah, do you hear?"

"Hear what?" She'd turn him a gloomy look and meet a face full of light and rapture.

And her heart would skip a beat with a happy premonition she was afraid to believe. What's happened to him? They gave him a bonus, maybe, and he brought it home in full?

"Well, what?" she'd ask with a little more warmth.

"Sarah," Uncle would say triumphantly, folding his paper with care, "a new blast furnace in the Urals! The country'll get another million tons of cast iron!"

My aunt Sarah was a very strong woman with a stern temper and at times like that she could have killed him. But after so many years with the man she knew better than anyone else what he was and how he couldn't be any different. Go ahead and kill him. What good would it do? He was an honest man, the most honest; the only thing he wanted for people was good.

He didn't want to see reality. It distorted his idea of life, tripped him up and, like a regrettable obstacle, stood in his way to communism. So he didn't notice it. On purpose.

I don't know what Simcha Kavalerchik thought about Stalin's having thousands of Communists shot for treason, when they were the very ones who had established Soviet power and put him in charge in the first place. You had to assume he believed what they said in the papers, and that for him they *were* enemies of the people. If he hadn't he would have said so. Out loud. He never made compromises and he wasn't afraid of getting into trouble. Then, of course, he would have shared their fate.

He kept on believing. Blind to everything around him. In spite of it all. What was happening, though, was wrong, and it was moving his way.

The persecutions of the Jews began. He'd have to wake up now, you'd think. His own daughter, Jeanna, named in honor of the Revolution, finished school and wanted to enter the institute. And even though she passed all the exams, they wouldn't let her in. They weren't ashamed to tell her why, either: Jewish.

Crying and moaning at home. Aunt Sarah pleads with him.

"Go. Talk to them. You're an old Communist. They owe you so much. Didn't you earn your daughter the right to an education?"

Simcha listens to it all with a face of stone.

"No!" banging his dry fist on the table. "It's all a lie. She had to be weaker than the rest. There will be no special privileges for my daughter. She'll be treated the same as the others."

They say money decided everything in the country. For a high-enough price, you could even buy your way out of anti-Semitism.

The next year they took Jeanna into the teaching institute. Her relatives suffered a little, made an effort, and collected a large sum of money for Aunt Sarah to slip to the right party.

When Jeanna came home from the exams, crying out the news that she'd been accepted, my uncle was the first to congratulate her, from the bottom of his heart.

"Sarah, you see," he told her joyfully, "what did I tell you? The truth always wins out."

The family turned their backs on him. He was alone now, a stranger to this world. It had its own life entirely, one he just wouldn't notice. All alone and he didn't even feel it. That's the main thing. Communism was before him, a sacred goal, and he headed straight for it, without so much as a sideways glance, thinking all the others marched behind. He went by himself though, blissfully unaware that he was all alone.

Along the path his own son fell. Marlen—so named in honor of the captains of the proletariat, Marx and Lenin. That's when Uncle stopped short in his tracks and came crashing down.

Marlen took after his mother and grew up healthy and strong as an oak. He was always playing soccer or skimming on the ice with the hockey team. The bones of the other teams would crack like nuts when they knocked against him. It was time to send the boy to work, and Aunt Sarah asked her husband to fix him up at the Meat Packing Plant.

"All right," Uncle agreed. "But no special privileges. The same as everybody. He'll come on as a regular worker, get a worker's training, and be like all the rest."

No one was going to argue the point. And so, as the saying goes, Marlen enriched the ranks of the working class.

Soon after, Simcha watches his own dinner table swell with riches. He eats tasty pieces of meat, he slices tempting little links of dry sausage, he holds forth at the dinner table.

"Sarah, see for yourself. Life gets better every day. Even this sausage," he says, raising some high on his fork and looking at it with love in his eyes. "We produce it for export and it's on my table already. They've distributed it on a wider market, and soon everybody in the country will have more than enough."

Wife, son, and daughter stare at their plates.

Simcha ate and extolled. If he hadn't been eating well, he never would have had the strength to fight the workers at the plant who were walking off with everything they could get their hands on. My uncle was shocked at their lack of political consciousness. Day and night he pleaded with them: Don't steal, don't disgrace the honor of Soviet man, the builder of communism.

And then, one day, he stopped in midsentence and never spoke again.

The armed guards at the gate never frisked Marlen. Out of respect for his father this was. How could they? But a new guard had come on the job to replace one who'd been sentenced for stealing, and with no understanding what's what, he searched Marlen along with everyone else. I hope you've already guessed "what was unveiled," as they say, "to his thunderstruck gaze." From the pants of this Marlen, so named in honor of the captains of the world proletariat, Marx and Lenin, the guard shook out twenty pounds of dry export sausage. The very stuff my uncle Simcha Kavalerchik had been eating for dinner. Simcha, the hundred per cent Bolshevik, who'd never suspected a thing and even seen the sausages as a sign that the gleaming peaks of communism were getting nearer all the time. Like the rabbi who stuffed his cheeks with lard, thinking it was kosher chicken.

When Uncle learned what had happened, he dropped dead. Right on the spot.

For his father's sake they didn't prosecute Marlen. They just gave him the sack.

Simcha, however, got a solemn funeral with lots of pomp.

The day of the ceremony a lot of people saw for the first time how many decorations and medals he'd earned serving the cause of the Revolution. They carried each one on a separate scarlet cushion, and the procession of bearers stretched for half a block in front of the coffin.

That was everything he'd ever earned. Nothing even left to bury him in. You can't dress a corpse in the patched and re-patched old rags he's worn out from the war, and there was nothing else in the house.

So, for the first time in his life, or rather now he couldn't no-tice it any longer, they dressed Simcha up in a stylish new suit. At public expense. The Meat Packing Plant didn't grudge him a penny, and with money from the union fund they bought him a fine black jacket and pants, a white shirt, and even a tie.

There he lay in the red coffin, lost in his suit. My uncle had been a small man all his life, and death makes you even smaller. Not to skimp, though, they bought a huge suit and my uncle rested in it like a madman in a strait jacket. The sleeves were half a meter too long and trailed from his fingers as they lay crossed on his chest. The ends trembled like black wings when they carried the coffin off.

A brass band played a revolutionary march. Crowds of people followed the coffin. The butchers of the plant went in the first few rows, their necks red with surplus energy. All his life Simcha had worked unstintingly to enlist them in the Communist faith. All his life he'd implored them not to steal, to tighten their belts and wait for a brighter future. But they wanted to live right now. Yes, they respected my uncle for his honesty, but they couldn't do a thing with themselves. And they stole. Every day.

Now, tears flowed down their fat, red cheeks.

The band roared its revolutionary marches, and it was enough to break your heart.

What more can I tell you?

Maybe nothing's best.

Why There's No Heaven On Earth
Legend Number Two

Rochl was her name. The Russian for it sounds a little different: Rachil.

That's all? A Jew with just one name? On our street this wasn't a person or even half of one. Just so they wouldn't mistake you for someone with the same name, they'd add all your parents' names to your own. More often than not, though, a nickname was what you got, and it would stick to you till the day you died. Even after, when they'd reminisce, they'd use your nickname as easily as they would your real one. That's the way they did it in our grandfathers' day, maybe even earlier, and who are we to go around changing a good thing?

So, they didn't call her just Rochl—that would have been disrespectful—but Rochl Elke-Chanes or, to give you the Russian, "Rachil, daughter of Elke-Chana." Elke-Chaneh was her mother, you see. Fair and square. No normal individual from Invalid Street would ever call a woman by her family name; that you could count on.

Her they did, though. Sometimes. But then she was not an ordinary woman; she was a "public-spirited person." What that means I'll tell you later. Let's just say for now that, unlike the rest of our women, she never lifted a finger at home, while her husband, Nachman Lifschitz, the *balagula*, a big man and, as they say in arithmetic, gentle and quiet in inverse proportion, would haul logs and 120-pound sacks all day long and still have to clean the rooms, do the wash, and cook dinner for five daughters, each of them as big as their papa and as full of the makings of public-spirited persons as their mama.

In official matters Rochl Elke-Chanes went by the name of Comrade Lifschitz. A term she liked a lot. She'd even stop eating her sunflower seeds, which she was never without, brush away the chain of husks from her lips, and answer you right back in Russian. "I'm listening," she'd say. With that she'd practically exhaust her whole supply of Russian. Still, it was enough to make you feel a little insecure.

She got even more pleasure out of being called Madame Lifschitz. There was only one person on Invalid Street who obliged her, though. A priest's wife. That's right, you heard. On our street of all places, encircled by Jews, there once lived an Orthodox Russian priest. This all happened before I was born. They might have sent him our way just to remind us we were living in a Russian state, "And don't you Jews forget it." I have a different theory, though. The way I see it, this priest knew which side his bread was buttered on, so when he had to choose himself a place to live, he came to stay with us. Naturally. Where in the world was he going to find better? And that's not all. I'm only supposing, of course, but I think that once he'd settled in the midst of the most inveterate kind of Jew you'll ever find, this priest nurtured a plan in the pit of his soul of converting each and every one. Like most plans this one also came to nothing. Either because it wasn't that easy fraternizing with our Jews, after all, or because the Revolution came along and, as you'd expect from a revolution, the priest was shot.

Only the wife remained, all alone, shut off in the house from the rest of Invalid Street by thick, old acacias. I always remember her as an old lady, dressed in the same, dark, antediluvian plush coat she'd already worn bald in some places, her head covered by a black kerchief, like a nun. She started warming up to the Jews after the Revolution and would be the first to say hello. The Jews even came to love her as one of the sights of the street. I'd like to see another street with a priest's wife of its own. We had everything on ours, even a Mrs. Priest.

Afraid of getting the same deal from the Bolsheviks as her husband did, the priest's wife showed a lot of loyalty to the New Order and participated actively, selflessly even, in community affairs. Let me give you an example. Can you name me one normal individual willing to let his own yard, garden and all, be dug up for a bomb shelter during an air-raid drill for the Mutual Assistance Society for the Civil and Chemical Defense of the U.S.S.R.? Well, they'd dig it right in the priest's wife's yard and not only wouldn't she object, she'd even slip a gas mask and goggles over her head. When the practice sirens wailed in town, there she'd be in her dark kerchief and coat, a Red Cross armband on her sleeve—still a cross, even if a Red one— inviting the Jews into her bomb shelter like a perfect Russian hostess.

As one public-spirited person to another, she'd call Rochl Elke-Chanes, Madame Lifschitz. And in return, Rochl Elke-Chanes, duly flattered by the title, would point her out to all the Jewish ladies of Invalid Street as the person best prepared for the chemical defense of the U.S.S.R.

The priest's wife lived to see the Second World War. By the time Hitler came to town she was the only person left on Invalid Street. Some of the Jews had managed to escape; the rest had been wiped out to a man. All alone like that, cut off from the Jews who'd become such a part of her life, she went home, drew the shutters, and died of a broken heart. They didn't find out she had died till quite a bit later, by the smell.

To close the issue altogether, I'll tell you how they liquidated the Orthodox Church as part of the anti-religious struggle in our town, and the consequences that led to on Invalid Street.

Once upon a time the heavy, sky-blue cupolas and golden crosses of that big, old Orthodox Church towered over our town. In the morning sunbeams would set them on fire and bounce off to play on our windowpanes. Then you'd hear the sweet sound of bells. They'd wake me from my dreams when I was a kid and I can still hear them now. Those were the finest moments of my life.

It minded its own business, that church, and to tell you the truth our town wouldn't have looked like much without it. But you can see things better from the top and when the Party says, "Hop to it!" the people say, "Aye, aye!" So, they decided to close the church and pitch the bell, that 3,500-pound copper bell, right out of the tower. Not a sight you see too often. Once in a lifetime, maybe. By the time the news reached Invalid Street it had made the rounds of the whole town, picking up new details with each turn. Everybody was in a real state. Young and old, we all looked forward to the day—twelve o'clock sharp it was supposed to happen—the way we would for a great military parade. The stories we heard! They'd sweep the street, each version more stunning than the last, causing palpitations and chills along the spine. On every park bench, by every gate, in every yard, people would get into furious arguments: How far would the bell fall, how many people would they need to throw it, how many smithereens would it burst into when it crashed to the cobblestones? This was dangerous business, all right. Everybody knew it. They expected casualties; the only ambulance in town would be there on duty twenty-four hours in advance. If anybody got a case of twisted bowels in the meantime, he wouldn't get to the hospital, that's all, there'd be nothing to take him in. It would make your heart sink to hear things like that. The significance of the event grew and grew.

Finally the day came. Morning, actually, we still had to wait till noon. On Invalid Street preparations had been under way since the crack of dawn. All the mothers had decided that not a single kid from our street was going to get anywhere near the church. That was certain death. So, at the crack of dawn, while the doomed bell sang its sweet good-by, a wave of children's whimpers began to rise from all the yards of Invalid Street. In every yard every father at every mother's bidding was taking a strap to his own kid, preventively, so he wouldn't get the bright idea of running to the church at noon.

The first to wail, as soft as could be, was Bereleh Mats. His father, a loader from the mill, went to work before anyone else and was in a hurry to get everything done before the whistle. He flogged his son the way he'd pitch bags of flour at the mill, rhythmically, steadily, and with his own shrieks Bereleh kept time. Then three new whines rose to join his from the neighbors and more and more as yard after yard added its cries and howls until it came to me.

I won't bother you with any more details, except for this. At twelve o'clock sharp all the children of Invalid Street were on hand at the church, waiting with their dazed parents as the police pushed them back behind the ropes that marked off the space where they expected the bell to fall. And at noon exactly, just as they promised, it fell.

What a flop.

It didn't burst. Unless you want to consider a little crack not everyone could see, it stayed absolutely intact. And, to get to the main point, no casualties. A dirty trick this was, if you're going to be frank about it. The people went their ways without a word, disillusioned and deceived. Neyach Margolin, a *balagula* from Invalid Street, spoke for everybody, all right. "A lot of noise out of nothing," he said.

Want to hear another unique thing about Invalid Street? All its Jews had light-colored hair. Well, light brown, anyway, never worse than that, and when their children were born, their hair was white as milk. Naturally there's an exception to every rule. That's what a rule is for, isn't it, the exception? Once in a blue moon we'd get brunets. Like my uncle Simcha Kavalerchik, for instance. But then, as you've already guessed, it would be the sign of an outsider, a stranger brought to our street by the will of the gods.

They even say that the Russian priest Vasily, who lived with us until his execution, was a fiery redhead. No harm there to the general coloring of the street. As far as redheads went, we had more than enough. All shades, too, from buttercup to copper. And faces so thick with freckles they looked positively flyblown. You won't find anything like those freckles nowadays. At least I never have. There were huge ones; there were some small as poppyseeds; they were thickly spread; they were lightly sprinkled. A lot of people had them on the nose and ears even.

A pretty bunch of people lived on our street, all right. Strong and healthy, too, like you'll still find among us here and there, but so beautiful they were beyond compare. No wonder matchmakers were so eager to get our girls. No suitor would ever dare poke his nose in himself, of course; he'd stand a good chance that way of leaving Invalid Street a real cripple.

Any time we'd get to talking about beauty, we wouldn't have far to go for an example. My aunt Riva was such a beautiful child that one fine day (long ago, this was, during the Russo-Japanese War) a childless Czarist officer, His Excellency no less, and his wife rolled up to our street in a varnished carriage with a lackey in the back and kidnaped her, just like that. They wanted to adopt her, you see.

Now, on any other street you could still get away with a dirty trick like that, but not on ours.

The second he heard the news, my grandfather, a carpenter named Shaye, ran after the officer and caught up with the carriage. This was a man with eleven children already, mind you, who'd have had his reasons, you'd think, for not missing one of them too much.

The carriage was harnessed to a thoroughbred English trotter. Grandfather outstripped the trotter, jumped on him from the side, caught ahold of the reins, and tried to stop him. The horse was a thoroughbred, as I said, and stopping him once he got started wasn't too easy. So, Grandfather cracked him one between the eyes and knocked him down on the spot. He killed a horse worth thousands of rubles. Not in today's paper currency, either, but hard Czarist golden coin. They say that His Excellency turned so pale and his wife dropped into such a deep faint that Grandfather Shaye just yanked the child right out of the carriage, slapped her for letting herself get kidnaped, and took off. Didn't even lay out a penny for the thoroughbred English trotter, either. His Excellency hushed it up himself.

Ever since then, more than half a century ago, whenever our family quarrels with an outsider or we just want to show what stuff we're made of, we bring up that incident without fail.

"So that's what *you* say." Or, "So you think you've got something on us, eh? Why, do you know that back in peacetime, before the Revolution even, His Excellency himself, a Czarist general (general, you have to admit, sounds a lot better than officer, and anyway they're both soldiers, aren't they?) wanted to kidnap and adopt our Riva. And when he couldn't bring it off it broke his heart. Took to drink he did and hanged himself. And you tell *us?*"

Now maybe you'll understand what beautiful people lived on Invalid Street.

It was the eyes that did it, really. All of us on the street, with few exceptions, had light-colored eyes. Gray eyes, blue eyes, light blue, even green, with little red spots in them like ripe gooseberry. God forbid black or brown ones, though. You'd know for sure then you weren't dealing with one of us.

It was Neyach Margolin, the *balagula,* who defined the species of inhabitant on Invalid Street. With all the literature in the world to choose from, the only thing Neyach Margolin ever read was a booklet on the great horticulturist Ivan Michurin. Margolin had a garden himself and used Michurin's methods to graft different kinds of apples to the same tree, a process which usually led to nothing. Anyway, this is what he said.

"These are Michurin Jews, all right, bitter to the taste. You know what they say: Take one bite and you choke to death."

Bereleh Mats, my childhood friend, was the fruit of a bad graft. Not enough that he was small and stunted like some tree in Neyach Margolin's back yard, he was a brunet too. His forehead was so covered with black hair he barely had room left to show you where his thinking came from. Even though they always clipped him bald, a brunet he stayed in that noisy, white-topped crowd of Invalid Street.

To make up for it, though, Bereleh Mats had eyes beyond compare. A light-green one, one of ours, that is, and a brown one, dark as a ripe cherry and clearly from another garden—I mean street.

There was a lot of talk about this. Sighing and shaking their heads, the women decided that it was the upshot of a vile disease that had struck a good-for-nothing ancestor of his sometime or other. Maybe a hundred years ago, maybe two hundred. Sooner or later the butter floats to the top of the soup. Although by Soviet law no son answers for a father and even less for a great-grandfather, they pitied Bereleh Mats like a cripple.

This to me is the purest kind of slander. What won't people stoop to? At least we didn't start the rumor. Suppose a neighbor's cow dies. It makes you feel a little good, doesn't it? Well, that's just the way it was with Bereleh Mats.

You don't have to be a genius to figure out why his eyes were different. It was as simple as this: Bereleh's father, Ele-Haim Mats, the hauler from the mill, was from our street. That took care of one eye, the green one. For a wife he took an outsider, a shortish brunette with a hairy brow. That's where the second eye came from, along with all the rest of Bereleh's troubles, like the shortness, the missing forehead, and the dark hair roots even after they'd clipped him bald.

Bereleh means bear cub in Yiddish, but they all called him *Meizeleh*, the little mouse. It made sense. Small and black, he looked an awful lot like an underdeveloped mouse.

On our street Bereleh held a rather unusual position. A dual one I'd even call it. On the one hand, our mothers used to hold him up to us as a shining example. He got straight A's in school and as if that weren't enough, he'd rush off to music school every day with a little violin in a black case and clean up there too—nothing but A's. On the other hand, our mothers all strictly forbid us from ever making friends with him. In fact, they kept us from him like the plague.

Beatings for kids were standard in every home. But Bereleh got more than his fair share. They beat him oftener and longer. His father, Ele-Haim Mats, the hauler, was a solid citizen who did nothing slipshod. If they'd beat me like that, I'd have died before the war and never seen the Germans come, as Bereleh Mats did.

I realize now that this was a unique human being, a rare specimen, the kind that's born once a century. If he'd survived he'd have turned all our science—mankind itself, even—on its heels. Maybe then the Soviet Union wouldn't have had such a long, hard, and always miserable time of it catching up to and surpassing America. Why, America would have capitulated herself and begged us on her knees to lend her Bereleh Mats for just a year, to straighten out all her messes.

Bereleh Mats had a special gift—he was an optimist. No shortage of them, you'll tell me, and ninety-nine times out of a hundred, optimism is no sign of genius. That's possible; even fair, but not when it comes to Bereleh Mats.

His optimism sprang from the great power of his gift, a gift that, in all its many facets, raged in his tiny body underneath that shaggy little brow like a fire. He was never sad. Even at times when anyone else would have hanged himself in his place. With every smile he'd show these great square teeth, and in his eyes, as the women of our street put it, a thousand devils would be dancing. When a man has a gift like that inside, he hasn't got a care in the world.

In the morning Bereleh's father, Ele-Haim, the hauler, his hand all rested from dragging huge sacks of flour at the mill, would flog him so hard you'd think there wouldn't be a place on Bereleh left alive. Ten minutes later, though, you'd hear the sounds of a violin coming from the house. And there'd be Bereleh standing at the window, drawing the bow across the strings, pressing the sounding board to his chin, and pitching a dirty look at his father's back as he walked down the street to work.

His father would be the picture of contentment, and his heavy step, with just a little waddle to it, would have the sureness of a man who'd done his duty. He'd flogged Bereleh with all his heart and with all his might, you could be sure of that. And the kid had got the point perfectly. Why, since dawn, let the neighbors eat their hearts out, he'd been busy with his music, and it does a father good to walk to work like that, with music in his ears.

As soon as he'd turn the corner, though, the violin would give a final groan and trail away. With a crash the window would fly open and Bereleh would tumble into the street, a thousand new plans glinting in his devil eyes.

If an ungrateful mankind had brought even a fraction of his plans to life, we'd be living in paradise already. But Bereleh left us early, and there's no heaven on earth.

"How come people milk cows and goats into pails?" Bereleh Mats once asked. "It's a waste of money on buckets. You ought to milk them right into your mouth and build airplanes with the metal you save."

No sooner said than done. That very same day he got to work on the first part of the plan, the milking into the mouth. Building the airplanes would come right after.

We caught a neighbor's nanny goat and tied her up by the horns in our back yard. Bereleh lay down on his back beneath her and threw his big mouth wide open. I squatted down and started milking. It's no secret that a goat's teats are big and soft, that they don't hang down right over your mouth, and that they swing back and forth when you squeeze them. Spurts of milk lashed out in every direction, hitting Bereleh in the eye, in the ear, but no matter how patiently he twitched his milky face beneath each spurt and tried to nab it with his lips, never in the mouth.

The goat started screaming—obviously she had no idea what this experiment meant for all mankind—and her owner came running. Ele-Haim Mats had his work cut out for him again. He flogged Bereleh so hard you could hear him shrieking all up and down the street.

So the project was nipped in the bud. And now it'll never come to pass. Bereleh left us early, and there's no heaven on earth.

All the women on the street had Bereleh pegged as a trouble-maker, a scoundrel, and a thief. Whenever he'd stop at any-body's house they'd hide the alms money they'd be keeping in the kitchen. At times like that everybody would forget that Bereleh Mats was better at school than any of their kids and knew more than the whole street put together.

Bereleh had a brother, Grisha, who was seven years older. Almost a grownup already. From his father's side of the family God had given Grisha an amazing set of muscles and, to make up for it, correspondingly reduced mental abilities. Grisha was just squeaking by at school and preparing for the technical insti-tute. Whenever he had to learn anything by heart he'd recite it out loud and twenty times over, like a prayer. With half an ear little Bereleh would hear his lanky brother's dismal mumble and remember everything on the wing. Now, at the age of ten, he was solving all his brother's physics and geometry problems. For his sister, Hannah, also older but physically and intellectually closer to Bereleh, he'd do homework compositions. To be frank about it, if it hadn't been for Bereleh nobody in the house would have passed a single grade. But it was the other children the parents loved and cherished the way you're supposed to in a decent Jewish home. Bereleh they'd flog like a scapegoat, heap-ing him with curses and calling down God's vengeance on his head.

I get it now. Bereleh was born before his time; people never could get to the bottom of him. He wasn't meant for the first phase of communism, but for its consummation. Mankind would really have rejoiced then. But Bereleh Mats left us early, and there is no heaven on earth. Communism, for that matter, isn't getting any closer either.

Why did they call Bereleh a thief? Because he was good-natured. Sure he stole; with refinement, too, and genius. But he wasn't in it for himself; he just wanted mankind to be happy.

Let me illustrate. Is there a child in the world who doesn't like "Mikado" ice cream, temptingly sandwiched by two delicate, circular wafers? No, there isn't. But on Invalid Street, where they'd stuff their kids to within an inch of their lives, the parents all thought ice cream spoiled you (nobody had ever given them ice cream when they were kids either), so for us it was definitely out.

And, speak about bad luck, there was an ice-cream vendor right on our street. Joshua they called him (Jesus Christ was the nickname), with his own handcart, rubber tires, and striped umbrella. Just the sight of him passing gave us a thrill. At times like that we'd have a pretty clear idea why they'd had a Revolution in Russia in 1917. We were eager to keep it going, too, and liberate ice cream as common property, free for all.

Bereleh Mats found a way. First he embezzled a little spare change from home. Then he bought as many portions from Joshua as he could and split them up among us. There was never enough for him. He'd have to get by on what we'd let him lick from our helpings. Grudgingly.

Meanwhile, we'd wolf the stuff down in cold bites and try to slip back home as quickly as possible. The reckoning, we knew, was unavoidable. And sure enough, before the ice cream even had a chance to melt in our bellies, we'd hear Bereleh's first shriek coming from the yard of Ele-Haim Mats, the hauler. They'd be flogging him for the money he stole. He'd scream at the top of his lungs, too. First because it hurt and second because, if he didn't, his father might think all his efforts were in vain and kill him altogether.

They took all kinds of precautions against Bereleh in his own home. Clever as he was, he got no more money there. That's when he turned his little eyes on the neighbors. Pretty soon their alms piles started disappearing too. We kept on licking Mikado ice cream, and now that the neighbors were lodging complaints with his father, he beat Bereleh worse than ever.

Once a Chinese peddler came to the street with a cluster of colored balloons, and Bereleh almost died. When you let the air out of them they'd cheep this high pitched little "oo-ee-dee, oo-ee-dee." We wanted one of them so bad it nearly drove us crazy. Naturally, that would have to be the time all the women of Invalid Street were mad about hygiene and sanitation. To gear up for the coming war, they were all taking sanitation courses and passing requirements for a little badge that read "Prepared for the Sanitary Defense of the U.S.S.R."

The Chinese peddler was universally denounced as a hustler of infection. Those "oo-ee-dee" balloons, they said, carried every kind of bacteria and microbe you could imagine. The *balagulas'* wives didn't give them a moment's peace until they'd chucked that Chinaman clear out of sight. He went flying out of Invalid Street like he'd been shot from a cannon.

Two days later the whole street was alive with little cheeps of "oo-ee-dee, oo-ee-dee." Colored globes on strings were bobbing in the hands of every kid fit to hold a balloon. Such a joy, and it was all Bereleh's doing. He'd gone and found the Chinaman some ten blocks away and with two rubles filched from Rochl Elke-Chanes, the party responsible for the little sanitation badges, he'd bought all his balloons.

Which were still cheeping "oo-ee-dee, oo-ee-dee" when

Bereleh's first shrieks rose from the yard of Ele-Haim Mats. This particular beating was a benefit performance, staged in the presence of the offended parties: Rochl Elke-Chanes, Comrade Lifschitz if you're going to be official about it, and her huge but gentle husband, Nachman. Knitting his brows like a martyr, Nachman blinked at every blow; to look at him, you'd think they were meant for him. Rochl Elke-Chanes, the social activist, Comrade Lifschitz herself, was taking it a little differently. She nodded with satisfaction, blow after blow, like a doting mother at every spoonful of semolina pushed into her baby's mouth.

She had her own score to settle with Bereleh. Just the week before he'd done such a job on the comrade she'd almost died of shame. In fact, she'd even been afraid of losing her right to engage in any further social activities.

The women had been busy in the priest's wife's yard, passing requirements for the sanitation badges. An important commission headed by the representative of the Red Cross and the Red Halfmoon, Dr. Weishinker himself, was supervising the exams. Rochl Elke-Chanes was in such a state she wasn't just eating her sunflower seeds—even on a day like this she couldn't lay off— she was gulping them down, husks and all.

For the medical examination they needed a guinea pig they could demonstrate everything on. You'd have to carry him on a stretcher, run up and down stairs with him, and get him into a bomb shelter. This had to be somebody you could save from burns of all three degrees, superficial and internal bullet wounds, open and closed bone fractures, the works. Any self-respecting human being would have turned the offer down, even if the entire sanitary defense of the U.S.S.R. hung in the balance.

They decided to take a child. In the first place, you wouldn't have to ask his permission; in the second, he'd be easier to carry. Even if they were in excellent shape and never shrank from a hard job, our women weren't too crazy about hauling around a heavy weight just for the hell of it. So the choice fell on Bereleh Mats, the lightest kid of all, and with joy in his heart he lay his body down, for the common good.

In their rush our women overlooked one minor detail that nearly ruined the public career of Comrade Lifschitz. As if all his great talents weren't enough, Bereleh had one more amazing gift: a chronic head cold and (parked right beneath his soggy nose) an upper lip that was never dry.

When they put him down on the stretcher in front of the commission, the nose and upper lip were both dry. His mother had seen to that. It was such an honor for her that Bereleh had been picked for the common good that she'd spent half an hour making him blow his nose into the hem of her apron.

Everything just might have gone smoothly if they hadn't decided to perform the complete Sylvester and Schaeffer Artificial Respiration Procedure on him.

Rochl Elke-Chanes, the first to take the test, dropped heavily to her knees by the stretcher where Bereleh lay, his devilish eyes wide open. She took his thin little arms in her mighty hands and, just as the procedure ordered, started raising and lowering them the way you'd pump a bellows. Bereleh took a deep breath in, and then out. The inhalation was perfect; the exhalation, a disaster. A colored bubble popped out of one of Bereleh's nostrils and swelled to the size of an "oo-ee-dee" balloon. Phenomenal is the word for it. Bereleh had never blown anything like it, not even in the middle of his worst head cold.

In all his many years of practice, Dr. Weishinker, the representative of the Red Cross and the Red Halfmoon, had never seen anything like it either. He started to swoon. Comrade Lifschitz rushed over with a glass of water to revive him. In her hurry some of her sunflower seeds dropped out of her mouth and into the glass and, to crown it all, they almost choked Dr. Weishinker to death. For what seemed like ages the women of Invalid Street pounded him on the back with their meaty fists, helping him back to his senses. He had to go on sick leave after that, though: back pain.

They chased Bereleh Mats off the stretcher and put me down instead. I was a good ten pounds heavier and no great fun to run with on a stretcher, but I came with a full guarantee on the nose.

After the incident with the "oo-ee-dee" balloon, Bereleh couldn't stand up from the whipping bench. Crying, his mother carried him off in her arms, bound up his head in a towel, lay compresses on his back and skinny bottom, and put him to bed. The tears were hardly dry on her cheeks, though, before her son's carefree voice came flying back up from the street. Nothing had ever happened, you'd think; nothing at all.

It was startling how much vitality and endurance Bereleh Mats had. Thin and small, a real starveling, with ears so big they stuck out from the sides like burdocks by a fence, an over-sized mouth that stretched from ear to ear, packed with enormous square teeth, the very best friend of my childhood, Bereleh Mats, nicknamed the little mouse, was a great human being, and that's the truth. There was no comparing him even to the top martyrs in all of human history, like Giordano Bruno or Galileo Galilei. They suffered for abstract ideas—how could you expect people to understand them? But Bereleh Mats's blessings were all concrete, the sort everyone could appreciate and we all embraced with joy. He suffered for them constantly, too, knowing that at every step there'd be hell to pay. But he didn't give in, no, and he never lost heart. That's the main thing.

Take a good look at those portraits of Giordano Bruno and Galileo Galilei. The eyes especially: what a lot of suffering, what self-sacrifice. What a pair of victims. "People," they seem to be telling you, "don't ever forget how we suffered. Thanks to us, you'll never be lost in the stars; thanks to us, you'll never flunk your science exams—. 'Yes,' you'll tell them, 'earth spins!'"

Bereleh Mats wanted no thanks from mankind. His own deeds gave him the biggest kick of all. What more could he want? If they'd saved just one picture of him for posterity, you know what you'd see? Bright little eyes full of mischief, a moist little pug nose, and stretched from ear to ear, both of them like burdocks, a big, big smile. If only Bereleh had survived, if only he'd had enough money like any other decent human being, so he wouldn't have to steal somebody else's. . . . Ah, what he might have done for people, what our poor sinful planet might look like today! It takes my breath away just to think of it.

But Bereleh left us early, and there's no heaven on earth.

I want all you future historians to pay close attention to what I'm going to say. Gentlemen, take down your lists of the greatest feats ever done for the good of mankind, and find room for one more. Be objective about it, too—this isn't the Great Soviet Encyclopedia we're talking about. Don't be embarrassed if the person in question is, alas, a Jew, or if his name Bereleh Mats doesn't sound quite Italian, or if he wasn't born somewhere in the rich hills of Tuscany instead of Invalid Street.

Just before the Second World War when long bread lines were already snaking their way through the Soviet Union, and to buy a bicycle you had to camp out in front of the store for three nights in a row, they had a triumphant Moscow opening of the first children's railroad. Railroad, hell, this was a miracle! All the papers ran stories and pictures on it and openly implied that the capitalist West had never dreamed of anything like it.

Take a minute and imagine it for yourself. A tiny little steam engine no bigger than a toy, little cars the same size, and all of them just as real as the big ones. Real steam, a real whistle, and an engine that moves under its own power with no tricks whatsoever. The engineer and the conductors are all kids dressed up in real railroad uniforms. And the passengers? Our age exclusively, no adults whatsoever allowed.

It was enough to drive you crazy. Stalin, the best friend Soviet children—or railwaymen—ever had, had brought joy to the hearts of the Moscow Pioneers. As for the rest of us kids, either he'd forgotten or simply didn't have the time. After all, he was leading an entire country down the road to communism back then, and that was no laughing matter. To make matters worse, the land was teeming with traitors pitching monkey wrenches into things, and they had to be ruthlessly destroyed, too. It isn't surprising that with headaches like that he forgot all about the children of Invalid Street.

Bereleh Mats decided to take matters in hand. Stretching a railroad line through the center of Invalid Street was beyond even his powers, of course, especially when it came to getting an engine and cars. I've told you already, just to get a bike back in those days was a big event. So Bereleh Mats cooked up a little something of his own. And it was so brilliant that, for a while at least, we had the jump on Moscow.

It was winter and the snow on our street was full of glossy, slippery ruts pressed by the heavy sleds of the *balagulas*. They'd make great rails. As for the cars, every kid had a sled in his yard; by tying them together you could stretch out a long train. The only thing missing was the engine. Bereleh told us to keep it quiet and be ready for action the next morning.

He made me his assistant and, at dawn, called me out of the house with a whistle. We headed down the street to the city market. Even though he was as lighthearted as ever, Bereleh seemed a little rattled to me that morning. There was a reason.

He'd just stolen twenty rubles from the neighbors—a real fortune, as Mama used to say of that much cash. Ele-Haim Mats would have to haul heavy sacks around the mill for two weeks straight to bring home money like that. Real capital this was and we both felt giddy.

With our pockets full of loot we passed by Joshua the ice-cream man's cart (Jesus Christ they called him) and the stall where they sold yellow-labeled bottles of sweet soda water. We didn't even falter. A hundred temptations in our path and, like men, we left them all behind. Straight to the horse stalls at the city market we went, where the snow was strewn with hay and steaming drops of dung, and the air was so thick with screaming you'd think they were chopping a man to pieces instead of trading horses.

To tell you the truth, with that kind of money on me I didn't dare butt in on anyone. I'd have been yanked right off to the police without a second's thought. Where was a kid going to get that kind of cash? Bereleh looked even younger than me, he was so short, but that didn't scare him. With a wink and a wipe of the nose across his sleeve, he disappeared among the horses' tails. I stayed behind to wait, my heart in my feet.

Why they didn't catch him, why they didn't drag him off to the police station, what kind of lunatic sold him that horse, it'll all be a mystery to me till the day I die. When I spotted Bereleh Mats leading one sold horse on a rope, looking so confident you'd have thought there was nothing to it, I just wasn't up to asking questions. I felt so giddy I didn't even notice the horse. It was only later, after I'd pulled myself together, that I realized the thing he'd just bought had stopped being a horse a long time ago. "A living corpse," that's what Leo Tolstoy, the great writer, would have called her, to put it mildly. An old mare, dead on her feet, half blind and so scrawny the bones were just about breaking through her hide.

For twenty rubles you couldn't have done any better. I understand that now. Back then, though, I was convinced they'd made a terrible fool of Bereleh, and I dogged the horse's steps, holding my breath, terrified she was going to drop and croak before she could even limp her way to Invalid Street.

My friend Bereleh Mats was glowing with satisfaction, though. They'd slipped a thick rope over the mare's scrawny neck and Bereleh held it by the end, leading her triumphantly down the very center of the street. The few passersby who saw us looked bewildered.

It was a day of rest. The men of Invalid Street would be sleeping late while their wives were at the market, hollering and haggling with the peasants over every penny. That was the only reason we got home without being spotted.

I ran for my sled and the rest of the maniacs dragged out theirs. Bereleh Mats was the only kid who didn't have one. His father had decided that sleds were an inadmissible luxury; they'd only spoil you rotten. So, Bereleh Mats was the unanimous choice for engineer. We gave him a hand clambering up the horse's ribs to its prickly spine and he pulled on the rope that did for a rein. He let loose with a hoarse whistle, just like a real steam engine, and that long train of twenty sleds started right off down the middle of Invalid Street.

This was ecstasy. We were howling, we were squealing with delight. Engineer Bereleh Mats had the greatest time of all up there on the horse's back, sitting solemnly and proudly on those thorns—what a picture of efficiency! Like a man who'd done a good deed, he could lean back now and gaze with satisfaction on the work of his hands. Every so often he'd let loose with a whistle and a hiss like steam bursting out from under the wheels.

The only thing missing for the real thing was steam from the top. Apparently our engine had been overfed by its owner just before the sale. It pitched out so many steaming lumps of dung (all of which dropped on me; as assistant to the engineer I was sitting in the first sled) that it looked like a real railroad almost. We were howling hysterically and we thought our happiness would never end.

Unfortunately, there's a limit to everything.

Our half-witted squeals raised a general alarm. The last to appear, unbuckling his belt as he walked, was gloomy Ele-Haim Mats, the hauler.

How it all ended you don't have to be told. This time they gave Bereleh such a trimming his mother, Sarah-Echa, a stoic through all the earlier executions, dropped senseless. His cries were so loud and pathetic, in fact, they had to give tincture of valerian to all the other women in the neighborhood.

There isn't much left to tell. Cursing out his offspring like never before, Bereleh's father, Ele-Haim, the hauler, took the horse to the flaying house and got some satisfaction: five rubles; only for the hide, though. Ele-Haim made up for the other fifteen out of his pocket. And so Neyach Margolin got back the twenty he'd lost that fateful moment Bereleh had popped in and caught them all offguard.

Neyach Margolin took the money and, to top it all off, demanded an apology from Ele-Haim Mats for his son. This was too much. Apologize? He didn't even know the meaning of the word. He'd never done anything like it in his whole life. Neyach Margolin stood his ground, though, and the unhappy Ele-Haim Mats lost his appetite for a whole week afterward. He couldn't look bread, or even lard, in the face.

I could tell you stories about my friend Bereleh all night long till you dropped from fatigue. Even then I'd be far from finished.

But I'll limit myself to just one more. It'll give you an idea of what that boy could do.

When I said he was small and thin you thought I meant weak and frail, didn't you? Not on your life. His mother may have been an outsider, but his father, Ele-Haim, was one of us. Bereleh was as healthy as an ox and quick as the devil. It's the quickness, in fact, I want to tell you about.

Ever since I could remember we'd had a problem in town with bread. First, they'd sell it by ration card, the quota and no more; then, with the victory of socialism throughout the land they liquidated the cards and you could buy as much bread as you wanted as long as you were willing to wait for it in an endless line forever. Around the time of my story, just before the Second World War, they'd run low on bread again, but they still hadn't brought back the cards. They were selling only one loaf to a man—barely enough to feed a tooth on Invalid Street. Even that would have been all right, though. You come, you get your bread, you don't expect it to be all that good, either. What —you want them to thank you for it, too?

But what you really had to do was stand in line in front of some store, freezing on a frozen street from evening till eight o'clock the next day when they opened the store, just so you wouldn't be the last in line, because, if you were, there usually wouldn't be any bread left for you.

It was a terrible winter. The temperature was down to forty below and every last Michurin tree in Neyach Margolin's yard died of the cold. How could I forget it? The winter of the Soviet-Finnish War. Supposedly this was a rehearsal for the larger war to come. Still, it took every young man on our street and some of the older ones too. One of them even managed not to make it back alive. Died a hero's death, as they say.

Just think of it: tiny little Finland, a country, you should forgive the expression, you couldn't even spot on the map, had got the idea into her head of menacing Leningrad, our legendary city, the cradle of the Revolution. This Finland, this splinter, had a lesson coming all right, and the Soviet Union was going to give it to her. And how it swung its arms! And how it wailed back to strike! And how it missed! Finland not only didn't surrender; she took a stiff bite right out of her big neighbor. A country no larger than a crumb. This was beyond human understanding. We who fly higher, faster, and—last but not least —farther than anyone else were having our hands tied by a bunch of stubborn Belo-Finns.

The children of Invalid Street were ready to rip Finland to shreds. But what could *we* do? We weren't even self-sufficient yet, and here an entire nation from the Pacific to the Baltic was spending a whole winter butting up against a solid wall, the Mannerheim Line, that is, with blood all over, and it wouldn't budge.

They say this Finland is still around and healthy as an ox. And why not? The way things are going nowadays, I'll believe anything. There's only one thing I can't get used to, the idea that you can buy as much bread as you want without standing in line. To me that sounds fantastic, magical, a fairy tale. Go shrug your shoulders; don't believe me if you like. You've never spent the night freezing in a bread line on Invalid Street.

People would start gathering at the store by evening, all muffled up like night watchmen in thick shawls, sheepskin coats, and felt boots. They'd stand there freezing through the night. As if that weren't enough, they'd all be expecting each other to pull off a dirty trick; they'd argue bitterly and make sure the line was kept. By eight A.M. an enormous black crowd would have gathered, cloaked in frozen breath, eyebrows and mustaches (a lot of our women had mustaches like Marshal Budenny) stiffened with frost, everybody looking like Santa Claus. Besides our own people, *kolkhozniks* would have come running from the neighboring villages since they didn't sell bread there at all.

By the time the doors of the store opened with a terrible creak, not a trace of the line would be left. It was terrifying. Everybody mixed up like an anthill, bones cracking, women screeching, peasants swearing all over the place, sweaty, flushed people crushing the life out of each other. I still can't figure out how there weren't any casualties. Maybe people from our street didn't break that easy. The crowd would take the narrow doors by storm and plug them with a cork of arms, legs, rears, and heads with bulging eyes. For the first five minutes nobody could get through to the store.

Those were the five minutes Bereleh Mats took advantage of. Decent mothers were ready to starve to death, without a single bite of bread, before they'd send their kids into a massacre like that. I guess Bereleh's mother, Sarah-Echa, wasn't too decent. The only provider of bread for the entire family was Bereleh Mats, the little mouse.

You won't believe it, of course, but he didn't just bring back one loaf, either—he brought two. And he didn't stand in front of the store from evening on, freezing through the night. He'd sleep peacefully in bed, a portrait of Marshal Voroshilov hanging over his head, propped by a nail from which his father had hung the terrible swift strap. There it dangled, always in view, and always near at hand.

Bereleh would arrive with his mother at the store just a few minutes before opening, small, unobtrusive, and bundled up in a kerchief like a little girl. There wouldn't be a trace of the line left by then, just a large, seething, brutalized crowd. Face to face with the nightmare, his mama would turn to stone. And, like a little child, he'd stand there holding her hand. From under the kerchief, though, those little eyes of his would be scuttling up and down the crowd.

When the doors of the shop flew open at eight o'clock sharp and that cork of human flesh popped up under the pressure, Bereleh would tug his mother's hand. That would bring her back to reality. And each time, with a groan and a premonition of disaster, she'd lift up her son and mount him on the back of the farthest person in the crowd. Bereleh would do the rest himself. Light as an acrobat—no, next to him an acrobat was nothing —like Chita the Chimp in the Tarzan movies, Bereleh would skim over the crowd, pushing off shoulders and heads with his legs. Right over the hats and kerchiefs he'd go, before people even had a chance to figure out what was happening. By the time they did he'd already be reaching the doors and diving through the narrow gap between the lintel and their heads. And he'd be the first to get bread. One loaf. He'd get the second by dropping back a few people and standing in the line that formed at the counter. Then he'd run off to school and get A's in every subject.

Before you knew it, everyone on the street had learned how Bereleh was getting bread for his family. No one blamed him for being dishonest, God forbid! Dodginess was at a premium on the street and people respected it. No, a different kind of emotion altogether was involved. In every home Bereleh had never been known as anything but a wiseacre, a troublemaker, a thief, and a vagabond, and parents would keep their kids from him like the plague. Now they started whistling a different tune.

"Why do parents have children? To help their parents, that's why, to provide, to bring bread into the house, but what can ours do? Stuff their faces, that's all."

That's how Mama put it, without looking me straight in the face. She had me in mind, though; I didn't have any brothers. She'd say it more and more often, too, never looking me in the eye, just off into space. After all she was a decent mother and took pity on my bones. Still, why did other people have all the luck and kids like Bereleh Mats?

On Invalid Street mothers were God to their children. I was no exception. I got the message and decided to take my chances. Not alone, though. With Bereleh Mats. Maybe then I'd get lucky and come back alive with a sweet-smelling loaf in my arms.

We got to the store at ten minutes to eight. We'd never seen a crowd like this one before—a real, seething whirlpool. Sarah-Echa, Bereleh's mother, hadn't come with us. After all, I could put him up on someone else's shoulders, too. We were out of luck, though. They'd been on the lookout for Bereleh for some time and now they spotted him.

"Troublemaker! Thief! Bragster! Don't you ever set foot here again!"

They hollered at him from all sides and turned their faces to him—not their backs, unfortunately. Otherwise, you could have run along their heads and shoulders and plunged past the doors of the store.

"Get out of here! Make him run! *Mamser!* Troublemaker!" And so on. This time the trick wasn't working.

Later Mama would say it was all my fault. Because I was a *shlimazl* and I never got a break. A quirk of nature, she'd say, that I was ever born on Invalid Street and into such a decent family, too. I was always out of luck and now that Bereleh had been stupid enough to have anything to do with me, so was he.

I wasn't too happy I'd gone myself. In fact, I was depressed. It was different with Bereleh. Even a disaster like this didn't throw him off his stride. With a huge smile and very serious eyes, he sized up the situation for a minute. His tiny brow wrinkled with the strain and disappeared altogether. Only the eyebrows were left.

"C'mon," said Bereleh Mats, and he took me by the hand. We moved a respectable distance from the crowd—it was already storming the open doors of the store—turned into someone's yard and passed through a fence to the enemy's rear. It was pretty quiet here. Nothing to hear but the pathetic howling from the store.

There was a window in the rear wall with a ventilation pane in the bottom thrown wide open. They'd stuck one end of a wooden chute in it. The other end slanted up to the floor of the van a *balagula* had brought the fresh bread in. One after the other the sweet-smelling loaves with the dark, toasted crust glided down the chute and through the window, right into the center of the shop.

The *balagula* pitched in the loaves by the armful, leaving the chute empty for a moment between loads. That was more than enough time for Bereleh. Tossing me his mother's kerchief he jumped into the chute, stretched out like a corpse, legs in front and hands along the seams, and shot through the casement, the loaves of the next armful tumbling right behind.

Half a minute later I knew he'd made it alive. Everything was going fine. From inside the store I heard my friend whimpering in fun. "Don't strangle the kid!" he cried.

Bereleh Mats brought out two loaves of bread, and just to be fair he gave one of them to me. Honestly, though, I didn't deserve it at all.

What can I say? I very seriously doubt you've ever had friends that unselfish in your whole life. Or hardly ever will. Bereleh, you see, left us early.

I don't plan to tell you too much about his last days. Everything I know comes secondhand. Besides, the thought of it depresses me.

Bereleh was one of the six million Jewish victims of fascism. And if all six million were even remotely like him then, for the life of me, I don't see how the world can stand it and still keep on spinning or how the sun rises every morning without blushing once for shame. It's beyond human understanding.

Bereleh's father, Ele-Haim, the hauler, was not a rich man; just a simple hard worker who, unlike the others, didn't have the heart to part with his miserable goods. When the Germans came to town he didn't run. How could he leave his hut and shed behind? They hadn't come easy. So now he lies in a big anti-tank ditch, overgrown with new trees, beside his wife, Sarah-Echa, the lady with the low brow (the one my friend inherited), the mustache, and the sideburns. With them lies Bereleh's sister, Hannah, who set the town record for the discus before the war, and Bereleh himself, a great little human being, whose loss the whole world feels so sharply now.

The only one in the whole family left alive was Grisha, the older brother, a young man with a massive, beautiful build and a set of biceps that had brought glory to the town in the crossbar competitions before the war. Even he didn't survive the family for long.

Grisha was a tank mechanic and driver in the war. When they liberated our town from the Germans he was there literally on the next day, covered with decorations and medals. He spent every minute the command had given him for a family reunion, trying to learn how it had happened. And he did. He found eyewitnesses, and they all confirmed it.

The way they tell the story, Grisha Mats's face turned black. He started to cry, a thing kids on Invalid Street stop doing by the time they're ten. He left his home in silence, got a ride with some passing trucks, and caught up with his detachment. People say his comrade tankmen didn't recognize the mechanic-driver. No matter what they tried, he wouldn't say a word. There was something evil glinting in his eyes. If they'd taken him to a field hospital he might still be alive today. But the assault of Koenigsberg was under way, and the tanks moved into position. Along the road they ran across a column of German prisoners of war under escort headed for the rear. When both columns drew side by side, a T-34 tank suddenly tore away from formation and rushed the Germans, crushing people, winding arms and legs around its caterpillar tracks. Mechanic-driver Grisha Mats was at the controls.

He was court-martialed and executed a month before the end of the war. A firing squad of his own brother tankmen did the shooting. They say they almost cried to make holes in such a powerful, beautiful body.

No one in that family was left, and I've never since met anyone named Mats. It's a very rare last name. Apparently it ended here.

I have a big favor to ask of you. If you ever do happen to run across someone with the name, please take a minute and drop me a line. It would lift a weight off my chest. It would mean everything wasn't lost. And then, who knows, maybe two or three generations from now, a new Bereleh Mats would appear on earth with his own little brow, big ears, and constant smile. Mankind could hope again and maybe, at long last, we'd have heaven on earth after all.

The "Mother and Child" Wardrobe
Legend Number Three

I can hear you already: "What's a 'Mother and Child' wardrobe and why the funny name?"

Not to try your patience, I'll tell you right away. Then we can get on with the rest in order.

I can see from your question you weren't living in the Soviet Union before the Second World War. Otherwise, there'd be no doubt in your mind what a "Mother and Child" wardrobe was, and you'd spare me the silly questions. Back then that wardrobe was *the* symbol of a normal Soviet life style and it stood in splendor in almost every apartment—room, actually, since that's all there usually was to an apartment. Wherever you didn't find one, you'd find poverty and despair. People would lean over backwards to get one of those things and rise to an average standard of living. I don't know what the story was in other towns, but with us, people who owned a "Mother and Child" wardrobe thought they'd been singled out by the stars above. They'd look down their noses at everybody else, like gentry on the plebes. And if a young girl got one as part of her dowry, who could ask for a better recommendation? God grant them all such a marriage, they'd say.

The "Mother and Child" wardrobe was the one and only standard developed by the Soviet furniture industry and, as things go in a planned economy, the demand exceeded the supply, significantly. It wasn't just a question of money. To get

134

one you had to line up and wait. Not just for one night, either. Ah, but then the pride you'd feel, the way you'd treasure it! People nowadays will never know the joy.

They're gone now, those wardrobes. There's modern and there's old-fashioned, but a "Mother and Child" isn't very convenient, it's not too pretty—coarse I'd even call it—and it's become a museum piece. Although even there you won't find it.

Since the war, for example, I've caught sight of one only once. A quarter of a century later in the Moscow communal apartment of my friend Ilya Silverberg. Ilya had inherited the wardrobe from his parents and, since he's an engineer, he'd held on to it. On an engineer's salary you don't exactly run around buying new furniture.

It stood right in his room like a living thing. A little awkward, a little bulky, and shy as a provincial. Yellowish unpolished wood with dim little glasses in the doors of the small compartment, the one they called the "Child," and without glasses in the large one called the "Mother." To distinguish the wardrobe from an ordinary box they'd installed some figured carving along the rough wood, the least you could imagine, just a hint in it of that age-long striving of mankind for comfort. Even in this harsh Puritan age.

The instant I saw that wardrobe a warm wave, as they say in novels, pressed upon my breast. As if I'd just seen my old grandmother, Chaya-Ita, gone these many years already. The Germans shot her back in '41, and since she was totally blind she didn't even have a chance to watch.

My thoughts carried me right back to the thirties on Invalid Street. What visions: The first thing I saw was a "Mother and Child" wardrobe being hauled in triumph down our street.

What a sight that was. People coming out of their wicket gates or watching from their windows, joy and envy written all over their faces. They'd be carrying that enormous yellow box, thick ropes stretched across it, on a handcart. Harnessed between the shafts and dragging it all along would be the handcarter (they even had a job like that back then), Shneyer. And how could it be different? Would any normal human being ever let a *balagula* haul a precious load like that? God forbid it should break. For this you needed a cart with big wheels. Then you could rest assured. In the first place there'd be a human being dragging it along and not some stupid horse without the least idea of how careful you have to be. Besides, you'd have the whole family walking alongside, right from the store, propping up the wardrobe on all sides and hollering at the carter.

"*Shlimazl!* Watch out! Look where you're going!"

The loudest shouts of all would come from the mother of the family. Sweaty, her hairdo in ruins, the buttons all popped off her blouse, and, special for the solemn occasion, lipstick. The lady of the hour. She was the one who'd waited all those nights in line, not these spongers of a husband and kids. She was the one who'd kept an eye out so they wouldn't palm a reject off on her with a crack in the glass or a broken piece of carving. It was all her doing and now, like a commander on review, she takes her due of compliments and open envy from the neighbors.

The cart clatters down the street on hammered wheels, the wardrobe rocks dangerously from side to side as the wheels go tumbling along the cobblestones, and the owners of the wardrobe, mother and father and children, heap a hailstorm of curses on Shneyer, the cartman's head.

And what about him? Like a horse, swinging his shaved head in time with his steps, he leans his chest into the tarpaulin straps, grips the shafts with his hands, and smiles a smile that's silly and kind.

So what's there to smile about?

136

He had his reasons, I'll tell you, plenty of them.

First of all, as I've just pointed out, he wasn't all that smart. "Half-baked" was the term they had for it on the street. Second, all that attention his cart was getting flattered him. And third, experience had told him that the railing was good-natured and mostly meant to call the neighbors' attention to the wardrobe. Besides, when the thing was finally unloaded safe and sound, his employers weren't going to grudge him an extra ruble and they just might treat him to dinner with a little glass of vodka on the side.

This Shneyer also lived on our street. Not on the right side, though, the left. A big difference, take my word.

The left side and the right were as different as night and day. All the houses on the right were high quality, built from sturdy logs and swamped in apple and pear orchards right up to their roofs. Tall painted fences and heavy gates cut them off from the rest of the street. The people inside were a lot like their houses, too: satisfied, secure, and in the pink of health. *Balagulas* and loaders, butchers and tailors, people on their way up—ex-*balagulas*, that is, who'd been promoted by the New Power to the Important Work of the Cause and had become Soviet office employees.

The right side faced the world with dignity and self-respect. It had only one enemy in the world, the revenue inspector. This was the one man they feared, this was the one man they fawned before; the second they'd catch sight of him they'd pitch a cloth on the table and get ready to entertain.

Still, the revenue inspector was made of flesh and blood. Enemy or not, you could get along in harmony with him and even break bread, especially if you buttered his slice. A living terror to all private traders, the revenue inspector turned meek as a lamb on our street. He'd come to appreciate the fact that decent, self-sufficient human beings lived here, who, even if they did cheat the state to make ends meet, would never cut him out. He was smooth as silk to us. Come to think of it, he even wore a silk shirt the *balagulas* had got together to give him.

The revenue inspector didn't even bother with the left side. What was the point of that? The poor lived there. A multitude of families with hordes of dirty kids, huddled together in old, tumbledown houses, the roofs rotted through and lost in green mold, the yards so small you couldn't find room for a sapling. We hardly ever saw those people. They'd leave for work early and come back late. Then they'd heat up the stove, fix something to eat, and fill the street with sour, rancid smells.

That's where the unskilled workers lived, the shoemakers who hammered heels right out in the chilly street, the laundresses, the maids. Meek and miserable people. The kids of the right side were all strictly forbidden to visit the left. God knows what you could pick up there: an infection, maybe, or a dirty mouth.

My uncle Shlyoma, who lived like us on the right side (he was a butcher who knew how to cut himself a piece from every slice he sold), would look at the left side and say, "It was for the likes of them we had the Revolution in '17 and they're as bad off as ever. Now the revenue inspector wants to polish off our side, too. So why did we make the Revolution, I wonder?"

This "we" business was no slip of the tongue or the bad grammar of a man who could barely read and write. My illiterate uncle Shlyoma actually did make the Revolution with his own hands. He even stormed the Winter Palace in Petrograd. He was wounded and shell shocked in the Civil War. And when it was all over he got scared of what he'd gone and done. Depressed and gloomy, he wouldn't even read the papers. The only thing he thought about was providing for his family. He was a former revolutionary who feared the revenue inspector like the fire, and it would take him two glasses of vodka just to find the courage to say what he did about the left side of the street and why the Revolution was made. And once he'd said it, he'd start to cry. As kids we'd be afraid to go near him at times like that, he might have slugged us.

The ladies on the right, even if they were squeamish about it, felt a responsibility for the left. Every August, before the start of the school year, the right side would choose two of its leading ladies to gather alms. For the occasion they'd dress up "in all their finery," as my uncle Shlyoma used to say. In the best outfits their wardrobes had to offer, that is. And that usually meant their winter clothes.

So, regardless of the August heat, they'd step into white felt, high-heeled overshoes, deck themselves out in fur jackets and hats that smelled of mothballs, and wrap up their necks in red fox. After putting on some bright lipstick and powdering their faces, sweating solemnly, they'd make the rounds of the right side with patent-leather handbags in their hands. Just as solemnly each home would ask them in. Even though they'd already seen each other that day, the mistress of each house would shake hands with them, invite them to sit down at a table covered with a crackling fresh tablecloth, and give them alms, each as much as she could. Anything less than five rubles was considered a disgrace.

Next, the ladies would take the money and buy shoes and notebooks for the children of the left. A tradition this was, and Alms Collection Day turned into a kind of local holiday. For the occasion quarrels were dropped, people got on friendlier terms, and everybody took pride in himself.

The left side would accept the alms in joy and silence and then, till the next August, the whole thing would be forgotten and both sides would go back to their separate lives.

In 1938, misfortune paid the right side a visit. All over Russia there was an epidemic of arrests. Invalid Street wasn't spared. In one night they arrested all the Party-promoted people on the right side, the Soviet office employees, that is, and half the homes were left without breadwinners. Poverty and despair crossed the street, from left to right.

August came. In its fear and terror the right side had shuttered itself up and forgotten all about tradition. But not the left.

Two ladies from that side, two poverty-ridden, work-worn ladies, dressed up for all they were worth in their frayed granny housecoats, their torn straw hats with the artificial flowers, and lipstick. Then they did the rounds of all the hovels on the left side gathering alms for the orphaned children of the right. I don't remember how much they collected, a little or a lot, but when they brought what they could, there was crying and thanksgiving on the right side, and moaning and sobbing. It went on for a long time.

So. You can never say Invalid Street wasn't up to good deeds. The rest of my story will make that crystal clear.

Come to think of it, life on our street would have been heavenly if it weren't for one thing: the women.

You won't find women nowadays like the ones that lived on Invalid Street. The wives of the *balagulas* were as big in the bones and backsides as any of their husbands' draft horses. Those vast breasts of theirs took up more than their fair share of space, too. It was no accident our women always found holes ripped right out of the front of any new blouse they'd buy. As soon as they stretched the thing across their shoulders it would split over the breasts. Since they couldn't always afford a fresh one, they'd lay colored patches looking like little roses and leaves on the torn spots. That explains the chest embroidery our women used to parade around with.

They were healthy and powerful and that was only half the problem. You know the saying that goes "God doesn't give horns to a butting cow?" Our women knocked that one flat. What a pair they got from Him! An absolutely masculine physical strength *plus* a woman's stormy temper. It made them dangerous as dynamite.

Neyach Margolin, the *balagula*, put his finger on it. "Our women are fire," he said. "If the stores were out of matches, you could get a light off one of them."

They'd do things undreamed of by the bravest men. Judge for yourself.

There's a black sheep in every flock. Meyer Shieldkrodt, the *balagula*, a decent, self-sufficient human being, had a brother Chaim—the very black sheep I'm talking about. A healthy redhead like his brother, Chaim was a good-for-nothing. For not wanting to be a *balagula* like everybody else, they ran him right out of the house. He went in for a lot of loose living, and years later he came back to town with a different name, Ivan Verbov, and a lion. A real, live African lion. Chaim, Ivan Verbov, I mean, started performing in a show booth at the city market. "Man Wrestles Lion" the poster said.

Not one person from Invalid Street set foot in that show booth. Meyer Shieldkrodt publicly disowned his brother and wouldn't let him back into the house, even though it was jointly owned. (They'd both inherited it from their father, also a decent, self-sufficient human being.)

Ivan Verbov stayed at the hotel and guzzled vodka by the bucket. Drank up all his money and the lion's food allowance. Sultan, that's what they called the lion, starved for weeks at a time. You never saw anything so emaciated.

Not that I ever saw it or cared to, but they say that when Verbov fought his lion you could hardly tell them apart. Ivan

Verbov had inherited a head of red hair from his father, Meylach Shieldkrodt, like a lion's mane. Vodka had reddened his mug and brawling had flattened his broad nose. Just put a tail with a little whisk at the bottom and you could have taken him for a lion.

Verbov would dress up in a worn-out, embroidered hussar's cape and dirty breeches coming apart in the thighs, sell tickets at the entrance, and admit the public to the show booth. You can guess what kind of audience it was. Lady merchants and silly peasant women who'd come to market from the country. To them Ivan Verbov was the tenth wonder of the world.

After closing the entrance to the show, Ivan Verbov would turn on a gramophone and while the cracked record shrilled away, he'd drag out his skinny, half-dead lion by the tail, set it up on its hind legs, fight with it, poke his head into its mouth, and, for the finish, pitch it to the ground. The lion would stretch out like one of those hides they use for rugs. A hungry rug, though. It would roar with a vengeance. In fact, about the only thing that kept it from gorging that shaggy head of Verbov's was the fear of alcohol poisoning. Every time the lion roared the merchants and peasant women would freeze with terror. They'd even come back several shows in a row in the hopes of seeing the lion bite off its trainer's head. All over the marketplace they spread tales of Sultan, the Threatening and Hungry Lion, and Ivan Verbov, the Courageous.

It took a woman from Invalid Street, his brother's wife, Yenta Shieldkrodt, to put an end to the stories and Verbov's legend in one blow. To save the family honor, she decided on a crazy course of action. She bought a ticket from Verbov, went into the booth, and when he'd let the lion out of the cage, made a big announcement to the crowd that the lion was so weak from hunger even she could fight with him. Then she ordered Verbov to let her in the cage.

Verbov got frightened, and for the first time ever people saw that red mug of his turn pale. Yenta pitched herself at the bars, but he pleaded with her to think it over. That lion really was hungry and it might rip someone it didn't know to shreds. The whole market gathered to the noise and the hollering. The men laid bets: Was the lion going to eat Yenta or not? Verbov pleaded with her; he threatened to call the police. For being such a swindler, she told him, the police would arrest *him*. That did it. Verbov flung open the door to the cage!

Sultan caught a whiff of the stranger, opened that big, wide mouth of his, and started to roar. Everybody froze. Verbov's hands began to shake.

Yenta Shieldkrodt went behind the bars, put her hand on the lion's mane, and gave Sultan a little push. He lay down and stretched out like a carpet.

Ivan Verbov high-tailed it out of town that night and didn't even take the lion with him. Or pay his hotel bill. They installed Sultan at the menagerie, and once he'd got a little fat back on his bones, he started looking like the King of the Beasts. To uphold the family honor, Meyer Shieldkrodt paid off the hotel bill.

Later, when they asked Yenta how she'd decided on such a daring course of action, she said that any Soviet citizen would have done the same. So, on top of everything else, people found out that Yenta was a regular newspaper reader who knew a worthy Soviet answer by heart.

This was the kind of woman that used to live on Invalid Street. There aren't any left now and may not be again. Not for a long, long time.

Their powerful *balagula* husbands wouldn't dare say a word

to contradict them. The instant their wives' tempers flared, they'd turn tail and run without a thought for their good name. Who did that leave the women to argue with? Only each other. And that they did every day, with relish.

The only water pump around was in the center of the street. All the women would go there with their buckets on a yoke. While the thin little stream spurted out, enough of them would gather for a neighborly conversation, and it always ended in a fight.

A women's fight on Invalid Street had nothing in common with women's fights anywhere else. Except at the start. First the shouting, then the exchange of insults, then the threats. The threats, though, were never empty. As soon as the words dried up, and one minute was usually enough for that, the ladies would get going with their fists and yokes. A fight would break out that would make their husbands' blood run cold. Our women didn't pull each other by the hair and they didn't scratch. They fought like men, with quick, thudding blows. And before it was done they'd usually have to send someone running from the fountain for Dr. Belenky.

"Go get Dr. Belenky." Easier said than done. Even though he lived right at the end of our street, you still had to get him in a cab. For all his good qualities, Dr. Belenky had one failing—he didn't like going anywhere on foot. It was only five hundred paces from the fountain to his door, but you had to run three blocks to the cab stand on Main Street and go pick him up in a phaeton. That was the only way he'd see a patient.

Despite his age he was tall and strong as an oak. The only thing that distinguished him from a *balagula*, in fact, was the pince-nez with the little gold chain he clipped to his big nose. Neyach Margolin, the most learned of the *balagulas*, used to swear that Dr. Belenky had perfect vision; those pince-nez were made out of plain window glass, he said; the only reason he wore them was to look cultured.

Dr. Belenky took care of everybody and never charged the poor. The whole street worshiped him. Not just for raising the dead, but for never acting against his conscience. Unlike other doctors, he always told his patients the truth.

Let me give you an example. Say a hundred-year-old granny from Invalid Street comes and complains she can only carry ten buckets of water from the fountain before her stomach starts to ache. Dr. Belenky asks her politely to strip to the waist. He taps her little ribs, listens to his stethoscope, and tells her, tenderly and persuasively, "Time to die."

Coquettishly Granny puts a blouse over what were once her breasts and tells him, like a member of her own family, "Doctor, that's still hard to do, somehow."

He pats her on the shoulder and "Now, now," he tells her warmly, like a member of his own family, too, "come to your senses and you'll see it my way."

Just like that; that's all there is to it. He levels with her and she accepts it. A heart-to-heart talk they have and no hard feelings. Not like some other places where they promise you God knows what and you up and die anyway. No, sir. Here you die quietly and at peace with the world because Dr. Belenky told you everything, and he's not a man to play you false.

Dr. Belenky's prestige grew even greater after someone tried to rob his apartment. The burglar obviously didn't know much about Invalid Street. The doctor caught him in the middle of the night, knocked him senseless with a crack across the head, put the stitches in himself, prescribed the medicine, and let him go with enough money for the road, so he shouldn't waste time getting out of town or ever show his nose around there again.

This was the Dr. Belenky who'd pull up in the phaeton to the watering fountain, lend some surgical help to the victims, and reconcile the warring sides. Even he couldn't do that much to calm the hotbeds of conflict on Invalid Street, though. All that excess energy in our women had to have an outlet somewhere. It was the husbands who'd suffer most for it, those good, gentle, powerful *balagulas*. Their wives would give them strict orders not to talk to their rivals' husbands. All the men could do, since they didn't dare break the ban, was exchange winks and glances and quickly turn away the second their stern, controlling ladies gave them the eye.

There was only one year, a little before the war, when all the people of Invalid Street loved each other like brothers and sisters, and peace and paradise were theirs. For a whole year there were no fights, for a whole year the entire street had the same concerns at heart, like one big family. As if they sensed the trouble waiting for them all.

Dr. Belenky was the one who dreamed up the occasion for the truce, and it was just what they needed to open up all the good in their hearts.

Here was the plan.

Living on the left side of Invalid Street in a miserable slum was an old maid named Stefa. She was over thirty, a redhead with a face full of freckles and, unlike the big-breasted women of our street, desperately skinny. Flat as a board in front and in back. No prize on the marriage market, as they say, absolutely. Meek and downtrodden, she lived on the miserable salary of a hospital maid. Whenever she went outside, which was rare, she'd blush to the tips of her ears at the first sight of a man.

Dr. Belenky took an interest in her at the hospital where she was washing floors and made up his mind: He'd commit a good deed. Get Stefa married. Her consent was a foregone conclusion. The only thing missing was a husband, and Dr. Belenky would find him, too. Right on our street, in fact.

You'll never guess who.

Shneyer, the cartman, that's who. The one with the handcart and the big trade in "Mother and Child" wardrobes. Good, downtrodden Shneyer, the half-baked. Lonely as a finger. He'd never even dreamed of marriage. The only thing the street knew for sure was this: Shneyer and Stefa liked each other and they were both bashful.

Dr. Belenky revealed the plan to the women of Invalid Street and, as they say, the idea swayed the masses. You can't begin to imagine how life started to change. The stormy energy of our women, that hunger to do good buried deep inside each and every one of them, burst through like a geyser.

First, since they were all taking part in the affair, everybody on the street settled their differences. The women's faces brightened, those sullen wrinkles smoothed away, and an expression of joyful enthusiasm glowed on every face.

Conferences were held in every house, women whispered to each other at every corner and embraced like sisters. Spontaneous meetings blazed up by the water fountain. And, through it all, not a single argument.

Little by little, even though they'd only laughed at first, the husbands got dragged in, too. For the groom they ordered a suit from the finest tailor in town, the one with the sign reading "Men's Suits, Military Uniforms, and Bell-Bottomed Trousers, Too"; for the bride the women sewed a trousseau.

Only two people on our street were left in the dark. The groom and the bride. Shneyer and Stefa. For them it was business as usual. He'd be carting everybody else's "Mother and Child" wardrobe and she'd be crawling on her hands and knees along the stone floor of the hospital with a wet rag in her hand.

147

True, people had been giving them some awfully interested looks lately, they'd been aware of that. Everybody on the street would be the first to say hello and ask how they were feeling. That had been nice, too, but they didn't pay it much mind. Who had the time? It was hard enough already knocking out a kopeck for a living without wasting your thoughts on marriage. Marriage, nothing: they didn't even have enough for a wedding.

It was settled. They'd hold the wedding in Neyach Margolin's garden, the largest on the street. The trees there were all "scientific," grown the Michurin way, with several different species shooting off the same root. And if Neyach Margolin was willing to let people trample all over his garden—the whole street was going to have itself a time at this wedding, you could count on that—then you can imagine what a piece of business this was for everyone, Neyach Margolin included.

Volunteers installed electricity in the garden and hung bulbs from in between the trees. Families agreed to bring their own tables and chairs, and after writing down who'd cook and who'd roast what, they all got to work preparing the food.

My mother, to give you an example, baked an apple strudel so big it wouldn't even fit in the oven. Everybody on the street said she made the best apple strudel around. Now she was more worked up than I'd ever seen her before. When I was stupid enough to tell her it might be a little burnt, I got it from her, right on the ear. I asked for it, though.

Huge bottles of cherries and black currants, topped with caps of granulated sugar, materialized on all the window sills, right in the sun, to speed up fermentation, and turn them into fruit brandy. Our dressmakers, who were at work on the bride's gowns and didn't want to let the cat out of the bag, nearly went crazy trying to figure out how to get Stefa's measurements. They'd use any excuse they could think of to stop her on the street.

Then, while they talked, sometimes by sight and sometimes with an open-handed hug or two, they'd get the width of her waist and shoulders.

The street was seething with activity and there was so much excitement in the air it thrilled you just to breathe. Tasty smells were pouring out of every window and—here's the main thing—there was a smile on everybody's face. Everybody was being very, very friendly. I discovered something then that was to comfort me in the darkest moments of my life. In everyone on earth without exception there's an endless source of love and goodness ready to burst out. If only things are right. Which, more often than not, they aren't. People lose out on a lot that way, on warmth, on love, on all the good things they deserve. And that's a crying shame.

But let's get back to Invalid Street. The day of the wedding the women swept the sidewalks. They'd been up since the crack of dawn already, washing their children's necks and ears. The main event took place just before dusk. Right after dinner our women got together to buy the newlyweds the dream of every family, the most expensive gift you could imagine, a "Mother and Child" wardrobe. It wasn't just the money that made it so precious, or even the waiting (you could bet that more than one person had stood in line and for more than one night, too). But to get the very wardrobe you've always dreamed of for yourself and to give it to somebody else—not so easy, you'll agree.

Ah, but then you should have seen the looks on the faces of those women when they carried that "Mother and Child" wardrobe in triumph down the street. That more than made up for it. And who should be carrying the thing but Shneyer himself, without a clue that it was meant for him. On he went, deafened by the hollers and the moans of our ladies, no less than twenty of them, who'd followed the wardrobe all the way to the store and propped it up on three sides so that, God forbid, the *shlimazl* shouldn't overturn the precious collective gift.

At every careless jolt of the wheels on the cobblestones, a woman's cry would slice through the air.

"*Shlimazl!* Vagabond! Convert! Watch it, ragpile! Good for nothing! Half-baked!"

Like hail, it all fell on the round, shaven head of poor Shneyer, the man they'd planned to surprise. He leaned his soaking chest into the straps and looked around him like a madman. All those people on the sidewalk, their eyes on him and not the wardrobe, with looks so loving and tender it made no sense at all. What the hell was going on?

Shneyer and Stefa didn't learn they were engaged till that evening when the whole street crowded into Neyach Margolin's garden with cast-iron pots and baking dishes full of Jewish cooking. The smell on the street was enough to knock you silly. On top of everything else, it was laced with the sharp aroma of mothballs. Everybody had taken his best clothes out of storage, it was such a big affair.

A joint orchestra from Handicraftsmen's Gardens and the City Fire Brigade, paid in advance right and proper, was tuning up. To the sounds a delegation of men set off for Shneyer's little room and, dressed in all their finery, a delegation of the most esteemed ladies paid a call on Stefa. And told them all.

They were both struck dumb. They went limp and let themselves be dressed in their new clothes. Next they were led into Neyach Margolin's yard, a teeming, jubilant crowd following close behind. There, under the light of countless electric bulbs, where hundreds of dishes stewed away in dressings, gravies, and sauces, the joint orchestra struck up with a friendly flourish.

They sat them down side by side, petrified and pale, and a celebration started the likes of which our street had never seen.

Later, Neyach Margolin put his finger on it, again: The richest man in the world couldn't have had himself such a wedding, he said, not at any price. People's happiness and love you don't buy—not even for a million.

Dr. Belenky gave the groom a personal gift right at the ceremony. A winter coat with a sealskin collar. They'd custom-sewn it for the doctor way before the Revolution and even though it was already pretty well motheaten, you could never find cloth or fur like that any more. The groom was swamped in it and almost suffocated (the whole thing happened in July, of course). Still, he didn't take it off until the end.

As usual (once things got started) everybody forgot about the newlyweds. Heads spun with the vodka and the fruit brandy. People who'd been enemies for years kissed passionately and swore to love and honor each other till the end of time.

They didn't seat the kids at the tables. Their parents sat in front of them and would pass them now a goose leg, now a piece of strudel, behind their backs.

The orchestra had been well paid and it played with all its might. To hear each other, people had to holler like the deaf.

All the gifts, and there was a mountain of them in the garden, piled around the "Mother and Child" wardrobe, stayed right out in the open. There to protect them was Gilka Knut, fresh from a year in jail for petty larceny. You couldn't have done better for a watchman. From the likes of him you don't steal.

Flattered by the vote of confidence, Gilka decked himself out in the patent-leather shoes he'd gone to jail for in the first place (he'd salted them away during the search) and met anyone who got near the gifts with the same laconic question: "Hey, you want a fat lip?"

It was way past two in the morning, long after all the food and drink were gone and the coordination of the musicians had started to slide (the kids had already gone to sleep beside the tables on the grass), when Neyach Margolin, the *balagula*, suddenly remembered they'd forgotten the main thing. You see, it was generally agreed that neither the bride nor the groom had the slightest idea what a wedding night was or what to do with it. So, for instruction, the *balagulas* took the groom off to one side of the garden, their wives took the bride to another, and there, with lots of heated give-and-take, they compared notes.

The next day practically everybody had a headache. When the street finally got up, which took a while, it went right back to the day before. Tousled and a little puffy, everybody looked out the window waiting for the newlyweds to come out of their hovel into the light of day. As soon as they did, holding hands like children, they got such a blast of greetings and sly little hints from every door and window, spoken for all to hear, that they blushed for shame and whisked right back inside.

Little by little life returned to normal. The street sank back into the same old worries. There was still the revenue inspector to worry about. He'd be coming, you could be sure of that. The whole town was buzzing with stories about the wedding and in the retelling the sums spent grew a hundredfold.

Even though the holiday was over, something still remained. You could almost say that the entire street had grown together during the days of the preparations and now those ties were being strengthened by new concerns. Not of the lightest sort, either. They had to do with the very self-respect of Invalid Street. Every day the women would look Stefa up and down, a real inspection it was, and gossip by the water fountain, and sigh and moan through the evenings by their gates. One thing stirred them all now; when was Stefa going to get pregnant? Sure, she was getting better looking. She'd be just like a little flower pretty soon. Everybody agreed. Still, not even the sharpest eye could catch the shadow of a change.

The men were more direct about it. They'd meet Shneyer with his cart and reproach him for being such a weakling. What kind of man was he, anyway? They'd offer to give him a lesson or two, even. Don't let the street down, they demanded, that was the main thing, don't disappoint the hopes of the community.

Clear into the fall the tension kept on building. Then, finally, everyone gave a sigh of relief. It was official, Dr. Belenky confirmed it himself. Stefa was pregnant all right and everything was developing normally. To see the whole street rejoice like that, from the bottom of its heart, you'd have thought it had felt a child stirring in its own womb at long, long last.

Now, new headaches. Every woman on Invalid Street felt duty bound to give Stefa the lessons of her own experience and make perfectly sure they were carried out. Advice? The air was thick with it and no two pieces alike. With such good counselors who needs enemies? Dr. Belenky had to step in and protect Stefa himself.

You have to understand what you're dealing with, though. Our women just couldn't sit by twiddling their thumbs. Their energy found a new outlet and bubbled right through. They started preparing the layette. The first serious arguments flared up over what to name the child. Heated arguments, too, but peaceable. The general joy and elation of Invalid Street kept on soaring.

No two ways about it, said our women. They'd have to transfer Stefa from cleaning duty at the hospital to nursing. "A medical worker." That's what they called her now in their conversations with people from other streets. They chipped in and had the hovel the newlyweds lived in done up right. Made it fit for a person to live in. Next to the "Mother and Child" wardrobe they put an iron rocking bed with a little mattress, a hard little pillow, and a new light blue quilt. For a boy this was. For a girl they had the same kind of blanket in pink stored in the wardrobe. You know what they say, it doesn't hurt to overdo it. Anyway, what's two blankets for our street? A trifle. They'd have bought ten if necessary.

Toward spring, when Stefa was in her final weeks, every family got the shakes again. What if she slipped and fell, God forbid? They'd spit three times just to talk of it. Our men had never been big on showing their wives much consideration. But when they saw Stefa making her way down the slippery sidewalk, they'd take her by the hand and lead her right to the door. Things like this we'd never seen before.

And then the day came. Evening, actually. Stefa's labor pains began. Saxon, the cabby, was on duty in his phaeton far into the night. A crowd gathered in the yard and when Dr. Belenky announced that it was time, they didn't just lead her out of the house, they carried her, put her in the cab, wrapped her up in blankets, threatened Saxon with every curse in the book so he shouldn't dare go quickly, and sent her off to the maternity hospital.

No one on the street slept that night. Some of the ladies stayed with Shneyer in the corridor of the maternity hospital to wait for the news. The rest of us waited nervously at home. Mama got up for a drink every half hour and my father kept on lighting matches to check out the time on the clock. Thanks to the two of them I didn't get any sleep either, and when I looked out the window at dawn, I could see windows shining in the early morning haze all up and down the street.

We got the first news at eight o'clock in the morning. It was good. Stefa had given birth to a baby boy. Over eight pounds. People poured into the street and threw themselves at each other with congratulations. Mama sobbed. A weight had just fallen from her shoulders, she said.

At nine we got the next news. It was horrible. Stefa was dead from childbirth fever. What a kick in the head.

The street emptied; it looked wiped clean of people. The houses shrank and sank into the snowdrifts.

I'd never heard a hundred homes weep and wail and sob and moan at once, and I hope I never do again. We were only kids then and we didn't understand it. But one look at the grief in our mothers' faces and we wailed like we'd just been done the greatest wrong in the world. That's how terrifying it was.

Days later, even, when people ran across Shneyer, looking so lost and dazed and lonely as a homeless dog, they'd start to cry and turn aside.

Stefa's funeral was the most splendid thing our town had ever seen. They put the coffin in a truck and thousands walked behind. To see them weep and mourn you'd have thought they were burying the dearest and most important person in the world, not the poor Stefa no one had noticed till the day they cooked up her wedding. From the bottom of its good, loving heart our street cried and sobbed and grieved that its common joy and common care had been taken from it so suddenly. The only one to mourn Stefa as a person, for herself, was Shneyer, Shneyer, the completely forgotten, Shneyer, sunk in black.

The child, fruit of the spiritual flight of Invalid Street, was still left, and every family wanted it for itself. Its father was alive, though, and for the first time Shneyer showed that even he had some character. The child, he said, he'd give to nobody. He'd raise it himself. That put our women in a panic. What would happen to the poor kid in the rough, unpolished hands of the cartman?

Dr. Belenky settled the argument.

155

Until it grew up the child would stay at the State Orphanage for the Newborn. Even if the place was meant for abandoned children, the baby would be sure to get good medical care there. And as for the rest, said Dr. Belenky, we'll see when the time comes.

People grumbled about it, but they came around. Shneyer was still against it. He showed a sudden furious fatherly feeling and wouldn't let anyone near the kid. Dr. Belenky's authority broke even him, though.

They took the child to the foundling home and before the day was out Shneyer dropped his cart and took a job there stoking the furnace. He moved right into that place full of squalling kids, to be near his son, forever.

The passions of Invalid Street quickly died down. Things got dull again and comfortless. Once again stormy arguments and fights flared up by the fountain; hostility crept up on the hearts of our women and won them away. Just like the good old days.

What's there left to say?

Just a word or two.

The war came. The Germans drew near the town and whoever could ran away. They evacuated the infants' home in buses and Shneyer and his child got a seat. But in his mindless love for his son, the man made a fatal mistake. He seized the child and carried him off to his own place, straight to the hovel.

They shot them together, Shneyer and his son. Now they lie in a common grave that became an anti-tank ditch, joined by a lot of others who'd had such a good time at the wedding. And what a wedding. We'll never see the likes of it again.

Who's World Champion After All?
Legend Number Four

Every street begins and ends somewhere. Invalid's no different. But while others start in a field, say, and end near a forest, ours, you'll pardon me, was in a class by itself. It began in a large and ancient city park called Handicraftsmen's Gardens. A handicraftsman's an extinct concept already. In plain talk, though, it used to mean an artisan. A tailor, for instance, or a shoemaker, a watchmaker, a porter, a handcarter, a cabby, even a *balagula*. There were independent handicraftsmen, loners that is, who were all heavily taxed. They didn't have it easy, but they got by. Then there were the handicraftsmen artels which, as semisocialist forms of production, were under government protection. If you belonged to one of them, though, you'd really have to steal for a living. Might as well put your teeth in dry storage, that's how much you'd make to feed your family.

The craftsmen all had trade union cards that got them into the Gardens free of charge. Half the town would graze there on the house. The privilege didn't extend to family members, so the other half of town, us to be exact, suffered bitterly. It made you stop and think: a state with no classes and class distinctions all the same. The injustice of it nearly drove us crazy.

The street ended—or began, it all depends on your point of view—at Spartacus Stadium. I couldn't imagine life on Invalid Street without that place. Every time they had a soccer match or a weight-lifting contest, our street would be deserted. Only the old ladies would be left at home, to mind the kids and make sure they didn't burn the place down. The rest of us would be at the Stadium having fun. The old ladies resented it, all right, but it never kept them from keeping up on every sports event in town.

After every match they'd be watching from the windows, and as the crowds came pouring through the street looking so loose and sweaty you'd think they'd just come from a hot bath and a great fight, those old ladies would rain down questions thick and fast:

"Who won?"

"What was the score?"

"How about the halfback, did he get away with it?"

"The center forward didn't blow it, did he?"

"Was the goalie dreaming again?"

Almost the entire Spartacus soccer team came from our street. All the players were Jews, except for the three forwards, that is, the Abramovich brothers Edik, Vanka, and Stepa. Pure-blooded White Russians they were, regardless of the last name. Not that they wouldn't answer you if you spoke to them in Yiddish. Gladly. There was nobody in town who didn't speak Yiddish if you want to know the truth. Except for the authorities, maybe. Russian, the official language, was the only thing that crossed their lips, stubbornly, and with lots of mistakes.

"All Jews and three Abramoviches." That's what they'd say about the soccer team. Like any normal human being from our street, the players all had nicknames. A little off color, some of them, not the kind you'd toss around in mixed company. But in the heat of a game when everyone in the Stadium was roaring his head off, cheering on or swearing at his favorites, respectable mothers, heads of families no less, would holler out the nick-

names in a bass and never even stop to think what they meant
or how obscene they sounded.

Want to know how crazy we were about soccer? Anytime we
wanted to remember the exact date of some event, we'd first
remember the game they played at the time and then the day.
That's how crazy.

For example: "My youngest, God give him a long life, was
born right before the game between the Tenth and Eleventh
Cavalry Divisions for the town cup. Three days solid they played
and it still ended in a draw. Couldn't change the score to save
their lives. So they drew the cup by lot. Pretty damn irregular if
you ask me. Wouldn't catch a self-sufficient person acting like
that, I'll tell you. So let's see. My youngest was born . . . wait
. . . I've almost got it . . . June . . . July . . . in August."

And he'd nail that birth date down, right on the nose.

Or: "My poor wife passed away in . . . when was it? . . .
Just a second, it'll come to me. Of course. The day Spartacus
played the First Air Force. Bulkin, the Stadium director's cow
spent the whole first period grazing on our half of the field,
peaceful as could be. When they changed sides the second period
she was right back on our side again, munching. Was that a
match! Total superiority. The ball didn't even touch our half
of the field and Bulkin's cow had herself such a bellyful of grain
she gave out two extra liters of milk that night. Let's see, then,
my poor wife died . . ."

So. Invalid Street began at Handicraftsmen's Gardens and
ended at Spartacus Stadium. Or the other way around. Suit
yourself, it doesn't really matter. The fact is that, as natives of
Invalid Street, we considered both those places to be ours by
right, and we could never get used to the idea that people from
other streets had the gall to go there.

Let's get back to Handicraftsmen's Gardens, though, the scene of the main event. Since May, men had been at work there raising gigantic posts and knocking together long circular benches out of boards. We'd stand there watching them with our hearts in our feet. Then one fine day, right beneath the tops of the old lindens, a canvas tent rose up to the skies. The Shapito Circus was coming to town!

I can't go on. I've got to calm down and get ahold of myself first. I was just swamped by a swarm of recollections, as they say, and one in particular: The time I suddenly became the center of attention of the whole street. Me, a street kid, a nobody, a freak of nature (if you're going to be perfectly frank about it and believe my mother). For three whole days I became not only the equal but the envy of every grownup, self-sufficient human being around.

That's all for later, though. First I have to acquaint you with the scene of the action, Handicraftsmen's Gardens. Say it was a good garden and you haven't said a thing. This was the Garden of Gardens. A jungle no less, its long shaggy lanes so thick with undergrowth you could sink without a trace. As a matter of fact, Rochl Elke-Chanes, Comrade Lifschitz, the main social activist on our street, had a lot of heartache from that place, even if it did turn out all right in the end.

Somehow she got the bright idea of putting her goat there to graze, to save money on hay. In the evening when she came back to get it, it was gone. High and low she looked and called with all her might, but no dice. That goat was gone. A milch goat this was, too, with a high butterfat. She'd even taken it to a billy goat a while before and that had cost her a pretty penny. To put it bluntly, Rochl Elke-Chanes, Comrade Lifschitz to you, was paying dearly for the sin of parasitism and for wanting a ride to heaven on someone else's back. It didn't become her as a social activist to make a confession, so she mourned it in silence, and every time she'd hear a goat bleat, she'd flinch like a horse.

Well, late in autumn, when the Gardens were bare, a watchman found the goat there with two kids. Rochl Elke-Chanes got them all back, and she wasn't even fined. She was a social activist after all, how could you disgrace her? That would be undermining authority. Besides, she'd been punished enough already. All summer long she'd had no milk of her own.

So there you have it. Handicraftsmen's Gardens. The only place our young girls felt safe meeting boys who didn't carry a pedigree from our street. Here you could hide from the jealous eyes of your protectors and the champions of your maidenly honor. Not always, of course. I'm afraid not.

Once upon a time a loader from our street, Hillel Manchipudl, the fiery redhead, found his sister there with a flyer from the First Air Force. The "Manchipudl" was a nickname and what it meant escapes me altogether. Anyway this Hillel Manchipudl finds his sister in the bushes with a pilot, and he doesn't like it. The flyer managed to escape: He was in the military, after all, and had the training. The sister wasn't so lucky. Hillel gave her one crack and that was enough. For a long time afterward she didn't even leave the house. Her mama told the neighbors she was indisposed. Migraine, the doctors decided. The neighbors just sighed sympathetically. Listen, they told their daughters, this is what you should expect from knowing a pilot, so learn something, it'll do you good.

If Hillel had stopped there, everything might have worked out fine. Except for his sister's migraines, that is. But Hillel didn't, and here's what happened next.

Like any other decent, self-sufficient human being, Hillel had friends. From our street, naturally, with the same kind of notions as Hillel on maidenly honor and the same kind of build.

These boys were oaks. They started combing the Gardens for the pilot in question. They didn't find him, but to make up for it they threw everyone in a uniform over the fence. After a complimentary poke in the teeth, of course. Not just pilots, either, but gunners and field engineers, even the infantry. With no favoritism shown any rank or arm of the service. Everybody got it except for the tank corpsmen. Hillel, the redhead, had served his active duty in the tank corps, you see, and he couldn't raise a hand against a brother. Besides his diplomas in Military and Political Training, Hillel had brought a new expression back from the Army no one in town had ever heard before. "Order in the tank units!" he'd say, not without pride and on any occasion whatsoever.

Anyway, that evening only tank corpsmen were spared.

Now who likes assault and battery, especially if it happens to him? I'll tell you, nobody. Air Force pilots most of all. Aviation was the pride and joy of our Army and people before the war, and the flyers just couldn't take this one lying down. Naturally. So, the next day, drawn up in a column and armed with sticks (weapons weren't allowed in peacetime), they moved on the town, right down Main Street, where the townspeople were having a promenade. Every Sunday evening people would stroll around dressed in their very best without laying so much as a finger on each other. This promenade was strictly a hands-off affair. Anyone hot for a fight, you could bet, wouldn't be strolling the streets on a night like that. The place for the likes of them was Handicraftsmen's Gardens or, in a pinch, the Proletariat Movie Theater where they'd be playing *Maxim's Youth,* the revolutionary picture, for the tenth time.

So who walked down Main Street on a Sunday evening? Old men, respectable heads of households, with their wives and off-spring. That's who. Self-sufficient people. And gentle? They wouldn't hurt a fly. Back and forth they'd stroll, everything nice and dandy, greeting each other from across the street so everyone could hear, burping loudly on a full dinner so their enemies could burst with envy, and, if they were in a really good mood, treating their kids to seltzer water with syrup.

These were the people the Air Force pilots attacked—the pride and joy of our Army and people both. Had themselves a time of it, too, heart and soul. Later an ambulance carried the victims off from Main Street (Socialist Street was the official name), crippled, wailing, and moaning.

After carrying the day like that, the pilots got back into formation and set off for the airfield, bursting into their favorite song:

"Born were we to make a dream come true
And overwhelm the spaces wide and blue;
Our arms are wings, our wits are needle sharp,
And we've a flaming engine for a heart."

Et cetera. They kept it up for all of five minutes. That's when they ran into trouble. Rushing out of Handicraftsmen's Gardens like a moving wall was Hillel, the redhead, and his friends, all of them from our street. On they came with bare fists. It just wasn't our style to use a knife or a stone or brick. God forbid. That would have been nothing short of impolite, disgraceful even. If you can't count on your bare fists, then stay at home and let your mama take care of you.

The fighting, as they say, was brief but bloody. In perfect military fashion the column scattered and scuttled its way by alleyway and leaps and bounds to its initial position. Back home to the airfield, in other words. Meanwhile, five bodies lay on the cobblestones of Socialist Street. All of them dressed in Air Force uniforms and all of them done in clean without resort to arms. Just fists.

The day they buried the flyers the funeral procession moved through town under an escort with fixed bayonets. The local police had taken to their heels so they brought in the tank corpsmen, the only neutral branch of the service (Hillel had been a corpsman himself), and they sent their own armed patrols down all the streets to avoid disturbances.

They carried the five coffins past the local hospital where the old folks pummeled by the pilots were still coming to. The sounds of the funeral march and the groans from the hospital windows mingled in the breeze.

You'll want to know, of course, if they all got away with it. And I'll tell you. Not by a long shot.

The whole incident had what you might call political consequences. The power of the Soviets didn't topple, of course. But a few folks did, all right, here and there.

Moscow dispatched the People's Commissar of Defense to town. Iron Marshal Voroshilov himself. He slipped in secretly, of course. Otherwise, who knows, spies might have ambushed him; all sorts of traitors might have sprinkled poison on his lunch. For us, though, the rank-and-file citizens of the town, it was no secret. Whoever kept a secret on our street anyway? If you knew something someone else didn't, how could you not confide? It just wasn't done. Voroshilov saw the incident as an attempt to destroy the indissoluble bond of the Army and people, and he was right. When it came time to deal with the authorities, he didn't pat too many heads, either. He made them roll instead.

I didn't see Voroshilov myself, but he was all they talked about on the street and, as you know, these were respectable, self-sufficient human beings.

They didn't raise a finger against Hillel and his friends. How could they? There wasn't a shred of evidence, not even a solitary witness. The whole street was in the know, of course, but who was going to tell on a grownup, self-sufficient human being? Such types we don't have, thank you, not at least on Invalid Street. And the same went for the whole town.

The Army, the Air Force I mean, her pride and joy, took full responsibility for the incident. A fair and respectable thing to do, we all thought on Invalid Street.

So, no repercussions for Hillel, the redhead? Since you want to know, I'll tell you. Yes, there were.

Almost half a year comes and goes, the *balagulas* are already changing their wheels for sleds, when retribution overtakes him. One night, some pilots lay in wait for him down a dark street. By the time they were through cutting and slicing, there wasn't a spot on Hillel left alive. And he crawled home! Splattering so much blood on the snow you'd have thought it was the Meat Packing Plant at quota time.

He crawled to the porch of the house where he was born, but he didn't have the strength left to knock. The next morning his mother found him on the stairs: both feet on the other shore already, as they say, but still alive. He'd always been a good boy who treated his mother the way you'd expect from a decent, self-sufficient human being. With respect. So somehow he found the strength inside for a last good-by. They spoke highly of it afterward all up and down the street.

Barely moving his tongue, the whites already rolling in his eyes, he got only one sentence out to his mama, but it said it all:

"Mama, don't cry, there's order in the tanks."

And then he fell silent for all time.

Oh, I almost forgot. The lady of the hour, the redhead sister of Hillel, the one in the bushes with the flyer who got the ball rolling in the first place, is alive and well. They married her off quick to an altogether decent, self-sufficient human being with three kids and so closed the book on the whole incident.

The town was upset for a while. Then it calmed down and, as they say in the papers, proceeded with redoubled energy to the business of building communism.

So what was I going to tell you? Oh, yes. How I became a celebrity on Invalid Street for three whole days without even trying. Me, a mere shaver, by the will of the gods, as they say.

Fine. But first let's agree not to rush ahead and to take everything in order, all right? Otherwise, I'll get tangled up and say something I shouldn't. There's such a thing as censorship, you know, and you have to show respect.

That year the Shapito Circus opened its tour in Handicraftsmen's Gardens with the "World Championship of Graeco-Roman Wrestling"—the kind they call "classical" nowadays.

This was a first in the history of the town. "World Championship of What?" you'll ask me. "Never heard of it before." Well, I'll tell you, I never heard of it either. Neither before nor after. Once I got to be a self-sufficient human being and an artist besides, a lot of things started making sense to me. For example: This championship was a sham, a gimmick to draw crowds into the circus. A trick not restricted to circuses. We all believed it, though. Not just us kids, but the whole town full of grownup, self-sufficient human beings. They were proud of it, too. After all our town had been chosen for the site of the world championship—and with good reason!

Posters with letters two feet high drummed the names of the fighters into our heads, each more deafeningly than the last. "AUGUSTUS MIKUL—TULA. Heavyweight," said one.

The TULA was written in slightly smaller print. It was supposed to mean that Augustus Mikul had come from the town of

Tula and would worthily represent it at the championship. We read it all at once, though, in a single gulp and it hit our bellies with a beautiful flutter as Augustus Mikultula. So mysterious, so full of promise. Like an emperor almost or a gladiator, and here he was in town, hot off the chariot from ancient Rome.

To see that championship, just to glimpse it even, what more could a person ask? Not to mention a kid!

But an invincible barrier lay between us and the world championship. Funds. You know what they say. "Put your money where your mouth is, kid, this isn't communism where it's all free. It's socialism, my friend, so cough up." We were broke, and the world championship was beginning in the next few days, just as the posters said, so hurry up and see. And who was going first but the heavyweights? It was enough to drive you crazy.

There was only one way out, or rather in. Gratis. It would take some doing, though. To get to the championship we'd have to overcome at least two obstacles. First we'd have to jump over the fence into Handicraftsmen's Gardens and then dig our way into the circus.

All of which brings up a certain character without whom no picture of Invalid Street would be complete. The watchman of the Gardens, Ivan Zhukov, that's who. He wasn't the only guard in the Gardens, but next to him the rest were babes. Comparing them would be like comparing a trained German Shepherd to an old mongrel dead on its feet, glad just to be drawing breath. A dog like that wouldn't harm a fly. But Zhukov? This was Enemy Number One and the meanest kind around.

Ivan Zhukov had been a celebrated guerrilla during the Civil War. When peace came it broke his heart. He missed blood so much he took to drink. He was the only man in town to wear the Order of the Red Battle Standard, right on his threadbare jacket, screwed to a little red circle of flannel wool. Zhukov had lost his leg in the war. Since they hadn't heard of artificial limbs in those days and he didn't believe in crutches, he built himself a wooden leg out of a lime log and shoed it like a *balagula's* horse, with iron. He'd run on that thing so fast the rest of us couldn't always get away in time. And we were light on our feet as goats. That wasn't all he'd do with it, either. He loved to deal out kicks with the fettered end like blows from a horse's hoof, straight to the base of the spine.

To top it all off, Ivan Zhukov was the only watchman allowed to use a rifle loaded with coarse, gray salt. Out of respect for his former patriotic services, this was. I had a taste of that salt in my time and whenever I think of it I still get this unbearable burning sensation right here in the root of my back.

With the nose of an old partisan, Zhukov used to figure out where we'd try breaking through to the Gardens and set an ambush there.

Once my friend Bereleh Mats and I had scrambled to the top of the fence. When we turned our backs to the Gardens to jump down, Zhukov let off a deafening shot, point-blank. We rolled back to the street with a howl and a moan. Actually, I did all the yelping. The whole charge, every last little grain of it, got me right in the rear. Such a *shlimazl* you don't find easy. That's the way Mama put it later. Easy for her to say, Zhukov hadn't shot her. Besides, she'd only seen me afterward when the salt was gone already, thanks to my best friend, Bereleh Mats.

Anyway, I dropped down to the ground and started rolling around like some halfwit. The salt was speeding into my bloodstream and burning sharp as knives. Without a thought for himself, Bereleh came to the rescue. What a friend. He pulled off my pants and got me right down there, wailing and whimpering, on all fours. The full moon, our only street light on Invalid Street, lit up my rear, all pitted with bloody little holes.

Without a second's delay, Bereleh pressed his lips to my rear, sucked the salted blood out of every little hole, and spat it out on the sidewalk. Passersby, and there were plenty that hour on the street, weren't the slightest bit surprised. They didn't even stop. Nothing special, you'd think, just one friend helping another out of a tight spot.

The only sound was the hoarse laugh of Ivan Zhukov, who was watching us with glee through a hole in the fence.

Zhukov hunted us down like a virtuoso, capitalizing on every last bit of his rich, guerrilla experience. He was just as good at blocking our holes beneath the circus. You have my word on it: No other watchman in the world would have found them.

It made no sense to dig a tunnel the night of the performance. That's why we'd do it in the afternoons, before dinner, when there was nobody in the circus and you could enter the Gardens free of charge. We'd carefully cover the dug-up earth with grass and mark the opening with branches. Here was the plan: If we were lucky enough to get past the fence, we could crawl through the hole beneath the circus benches when it got dark and climb to the top of the amphitheater. Then we'd come out through the legs of the audience and watch the show in peace. That was if our luck held out.

It didn't. The legendary hero of the Civil War, Ivan Zhukov, discovered our plot immediately. By day as we'd dig the tunnel he'd watch us from the bushes without interfering. When we'd slip away, he'd take a bucket to the public john at the Gardens and ladle out a pail full of dregs from the cesspool. Then he'd steal beneath the circus seats right up to where the hole would open and empty out the bucket. Zhukov used every trick in the book on this one. He even allowed for the direction of the draft.

The smell was headed inside, toward the circus. From the outside we never caught a whiff.

As usual Bereleh Mats, the quickest and bravest of us all, was the first to dive into the hole. He was also the first to start gurgling on a face full of stinking gunk.

Ivan Zhukov wasn't in sight. He sat alone on the open veranda of the canteen sopping up his vodka and waiting for his plan to unfold.

As soon as Bereleh Mats, smeared as the devil, and the rest of us roses dragged ourselves out from behind the circus benches and tried to disperse among the audience, they caught us. The smell was a dead giveaway. Indignant ladies called for the ticket collectors and in they came, all dressed up like lackeys. Holding their noses in disgust, they pulled us by the ears—the only clean place left—and pitched us out into the light of day. The shame of it. And there sat Zhukov on the open veranda of the canteen, laughing his hoarse old throat out, letting that third glass of vodka pass on down.

I got even with Zhukov. Not then, but years later, after the war, when I came back to town. I was a grownup, self-sufficient human being by then, who'd even managed to forget that Ivan Zhukov, the Red partisan, ever existed. I didn't find any of my old friends; they were all dead, every last one of them. I didn't even find Invalid Street. It had burned down. What they'd rebuilt they now called Friedrich Engels Street. I didn't even find Handicraftsmen's Gardens. Its hundred-year-old lindens had been cut down; only a little round spot was left, bordered by a new fence and strewn with thick stumps that had just started putting out pale little shoots. They'd renamed the monstrosity —how could you call it a garden?—Soviet Municipal Gardens, and you still had to pay to get in.

This was a real blow, straight to the heart. Even though I was a grownup and a self-sufficient human being with money enough for the ticket, I turned right around and went over the fence. On principle.

I landed on something soft that gave out a pathetic little peep beneath me. It was Ivan Zhukov. An old man already, he was still sitting by the fence waiting to ambush the ticketless hordes. His decoration was gone, lost somewhere on a binge. The only things left from the old Zhukov were the boozy red nose and the wooden leg.

I'd nearly smothered him, and he took a long time coming to. He was terrified. Later, when I treated him to a vodka at the canteen he drank a full three hundred grams before he got his tongue back.

Zhukov cried a drunkard's tears to see me. It really upset him to learn I was the only one of our whole gang left alive. Even back then, he said, snuffling and blinking his red lids, he'd noticed something special about me. No surprise to him I'd turned out to be such a fine, upstanding individual.

Then he complained of the way his life had gone. They'd dealt him a terrible blow, he said. New, artificial limbs had appeared from overseas. All the invalids of the Second World War were getting them free and they'd passed him over. Him of all people, who'd established the power of the Soviets for them at the cost of his own leg. Then for a long while he mourned the generation that was gone; when would there ever be another like it? When we parted, he gave me a wet kiss and started to curse. "The hell I need their false leg!" he said. "I'll see it dead first with little white slippers on it! I wouldn't change my homemade one for a hundred new ones. Fifty years I've worn mine, it hasn't broken yet, and I'll pull through a hundred more, is that clear?"

Maybe now you'll understand what that World Championship of Graeco-Roman Wrestling meant to us. As often as we could we'd break through and watch those thrilling fights. Not always, of course, but sometimes, anyway. Sometimes.

And now for the main attraction, the incident that turned me into the hero of the hour. After which, I can tell you, acting natural didn't come easy.

With the failure of the tunnel to get us into the circus, I made use of my last resort. First thing in the morning I started playing up to my gloomy uncle Shlyoma and looking deep into his eyes. Besides being a butcher, his regular job, he was a volunteer fireman, with a spiked copper helmet in his house polished so bright it would knock your eyes out.

Firemen got free passes to any performance in town, the circus included, just to be on hand in case a fire should break out and the public needed saving. They could only take the unsold seats, of course, but if the house was full the management would give them a chair right in the aisle.

Whether or not they were supposed to, firemen used to get their kids in free. Which explains why I'd been playing up to Uncle Shlyoma since the crack of dawn.

He was less gloomy than usual that day, so he went with me, all decked out in his fire-fighting regalia. As the two of us went past the ticket collector, Uncle Shlyoma raised his hand to his helmet in a military salute. The fellow greeted him politely without even turning my way. I was in heaven. I looked back and saw Zhukov, the watchman, Zhukov, the hero of the Civil War, standing in the crowd. I stuck my tongue out at him as far as it would go. He couldn't touch me. I saw how he suffered.

There were plenty of empty seats that day, so my uncle and I took the best, in a box right by the barrier to the arena.

Why so many free seats? I'll tell you. They'd just announced that on account of illness the main pair of wrestlers wouldn't be appearing. All tickets would be honored the next day when the pair recovered. After five minutes or so a lot of people went home. And lived to regret it. My uncle and I sat down in the half-empty circus. I wasn't planning to go; they weren't going to honor my ticket the next day anyway, since I didn't have one. Even Uncle Shlyoma went home during the interlude and for a long time afterward reproached me for not keeping him there. Better have nothing to do with me, he said. Honest to God, he really suspected I knew what was going to happen at the end of the performance. I'd kept it from him, he said, so I could be the only witness from Invalid Street. How could you argue with that? What was there to prove? He was a fireman and that says it all.

Anyway, here's what happened that day at the circus. It takes my breath away just to remember.

Down on the mat two of the most Godforsaken wrestlers you ever saw were wheezing away at each other—"in combat," as they called it. Augustus Mikultula himself, the one with the resounding Roman name, and his partner, whose name I don't recall. Something ancient Roman, too, or Greek.

"Ancient" was the word for them, all right. Augustus Mikul was an old man already, still earning his living on the mat. Apparently he wasn't qualified for much else. His muscles were all flabby and his belly was big as a drum. He was gasping for breath, he was so fat. *Balagulas* had an expression for types like that. "Off to the flaying house with him," they'd say, "before the skin's lost, too."

Fight, hell, this was a tragedy. It took a lot from me to sit through it, and I'm not sorry I did.

Both wrestlers locked foreheads like bulls and, clenching each other by their ruddy necks, they pressed and squeezed their bellies against each other with terrible force. They pressed and they pressed and they pressed, and it was beginning to look like it would never end.

And then it did.

Augustus Mikultula couldn't stand the pressure on his enormous belly and let loose an indecent sound with such a loud and deafening crack that to this day I still don't understand how his shorts came through in one piece.

First I decided it was thunder and raised my eyes to the sky. The canvas top of the circus looked like it had bobbed up and was slowly settling back into place. The audience in the front rows jumped back; the women blacked out right on the spot.

"Aren't you exaggerating a little?" I can hear you asking. Well, I don't even want to discuss it, I tell you. You have to be really envious to ask a question like that.

After the blast a deathly quiet settled on the circus. By sheer inertia the wrestlers made another move or two and shook off each other's holds without looking into the hall. To save the situation the orchestra on the upper platform rushed in with a flourish, but a few measures later the music went to hell. The trumpets started gurgling. The musicians were laughing too hard to play. Then the whole circus began to shake and roar. Afterward, people swore they'd laughed enough that evening to cover the price of a whole season's pass.

The circus was braying, hiccuping, screeching, cackling, and thundering away in basses and trebles, sopranos and altos. It shook the big top like a storm. They say you could hear the laughter all the way to the end of Invalid Street, by Spartacus Stadium. People rushed to the scene in whatever they were dressed—or half dressed—to find out what was happening. But they'd come too late. We were all coming out of the circus by then, still in stitches. Like hapless, Godforsaken people, they just stood there looking.

From that moment on my star was on the rise. Three whole days it lasted, till the curiosity of Invalid Street was satisfied in full.

No one else on the whole street had been there but me. By early morning of the next day my popularity began to grow. Not by the hour, either, by the minute. Grownup, self-sufficient people came to our house to see me, not my parents, and to hear every last detail straight from my lips.

They followed me down the street in hordes and gobbled up my every word with envy. Grownup, self-sufficient people shook my hand. Not with familiarity, either, or the usual condescending tone, but as an equal and even, I'm not afraid to say it, with respect.

A hundred times a day I'd tell them everything I'd seen and mainly heard. Then new listeners would crop up and ask me to go over it again. I grew hoarse, my lips got chapped, my tongue turned white. And when I was a complete wreck they'd bring me some Mikado ice cream. Not one portion, either, but two, and if I'd asked for a third to refresh myself before going on, that too. Mama warned the neighbors not to torment me. Otherwise, she said, she'd have to treat the kid with tincture of valerian for a week. Still, there she'd be, listening to my story for the hundredth time as it came unhinged in all my excitement and she'd look around at everyone with pride.

Three days the street lived off the details of my eyewitness account. We're hairsplitters—it's a national trait—and their questions wore me to a frazzle. Questions, questions, questions. All shapes and sizes, and not just the kind you could sink your teeth into in mixed company. Thousands of them, and with a head reeling from all that attention and respect, I did my best to answer every one.

Neyach Margolin himself, the most educated of the *balagulas*, heard me out and didn't even interrupt. This wasn't a man to give a listen to just anybody, either. He even asked me a question, and such a puzzler that it was the one and only time I couldn't answer.

"So, Mr. Eyewitness," asked Neyach Margolin, "tell me if you can, since you're such a clever individual, what did this Augustus Mikultula have for dinner before his performance?"

That did it. I was a dead man. Everybody wanted to know the answer, and all I could do was knit my brow in torment. What a disgrace. I couldn't even say a word.

"I rest my case," said Neyach Margolin, giving my head a flick with his oaken finger. "And you in school yet."

Everybody sighed in agreement. I *was* going to school, and the government *was* wasting a lot of money on me, and I still hadn't learned how to answer simple questions.

I stood there watching all those witnesses to my shame lose respect for me. Right before my eyes.

Once Neyach Margolin left, though, cracking his *balagula* whip in the air, with a look on his face that said a worthless generation was growing up not even fit to answer a simple question, my prestige started to rise again, little by little. No matter how you sliced it, I was still an eye-, I mean ear-witness, and no one had heard it but me. Me—not Neyach Margolin. So what if he knew more than I did or considered himself the brightest *balagula* around?

Still, as one of the greats once said, everything passes and glory isn't meant to last forever. Gradually people lost interest in me and pretty soon I was back to being a nobody again. It's hard on a man outlasting the peak of his fame like that. You know it as well as I do. He gets pessimistic; he starts hating the people around him. Well, it didn't happen to me. I was a kid, you see, and as Meyer Shieldkrodt, our neighbor, put it, I still had everything before me. He was right, too.

So why am I telling the story?

I could say, because. Just because. For the sheer beauty of it. That wouldn't be much of an answer, though, or, to be frank about it, even the truth. I'm really telling you the story to put you into the feel of things before getting to the main event.

Which happened very soon after at the World Championship of Graeco-Roman Wrestling. The championship was beginning to drag a bit, and the initial interest started to fade. A situation the box office feels worst of all. It's no secret: Finances start calling the dances.

So, to encourage the public to clean out its pockets, the management of the circus cooked up a little deal. They decided to invite the audience to put up a man of its own against one of the professional wrestlers on the mat. This led to some very interesting events, which I'm sorry to say I didn't see. That evening Bereleh Mats almost choked to death in one of Ivan Zhukov's traps. We dragged him out of the hole by the heels barely alive. We decided not to push our luck any more and went home, with nothing for our pains. To this day I can't forgive myself for that.

Whatever happened at the circus that evening I know only secondhand and from people you couldn't squeeze an extra syllable out of if you tried. A lot of details were lost and that's a shame.

When the *Sprechtstalmeister*—that's what they called the ringmaster—threw open the mat to the audience, everybody turned to Berl Arbitailo, a *balagula* from Invalid Street, who'd paid good money to see a fight, not to be in it.

Berl Arbitailo, to give you a quick sketch, represented the younger generation of *balagulas* on our street. He couldn't have cared less about sports, and it was generally agreed he was just like everybody else. No healthier, no weaker, just young.

We used to have a name for types like him. Big-as-Wide we'd call them. Every measurement on him was the same: height, width, and girth. He looked like a cube, all of whose sides, as everybody knows, are equal. Only this cube was made of meat and bone and the meat was hard as iron.

We have a custom. When somebody really insists, you just can't refuse. So, Berl Arbitailo went into the arena. Later, though, he swore he'd been dead set against it.

They took him backstage, dressed him up in a *bortsovka*, a wrestler's suit, like a lady's bathing suit almost, only with one strap, and slipped a snug pair of soft high boots on his feet. Then, red as a crab, he ran staggering into the arena to the sounds of a march. He even paid a clumsy compliment to the audience. Putting one foot behind him like a post, he bowed his bullneck by a millimeter. They must have taught him that one while he was getting dressed backstage. The *bortsovka* fit him so closely—they couldn't find a larger size—that all the decent girls in the audience put their fingers over their eyes.

In a pure, trained Russian voice, free of any accent, the ringmaster introduced him as Boris Arbitailo (Berl's the same as Boris in Russian) and added that he would be representing our town in the championship.

A redheaded clown who was in the arena at the time burst into an idiotic cackle. The audience didn't think the laugh was very funny, though. In fact, they thought it was downright offensive. From then on, all through the run of the circus, they hissed the redheaded clown every time he appeared. He had to leave town sooner than expected. Even changed his line of work, they say.

Here's what happened next. Berl, now Boris, Arbitailo gave his opponent, a real, professional wrestler, exactly five seconds to think things over. Traditionally, wrestlers shake hands first. Once he'd gripped him by the hand, Berl didn't let his opponent go. He grunted, arched him like a feather through the air, flung him on his shoulder blades, and pinned him as he stood.

The hall exploded. The canvas top nearly flew off to the trees. It was a clear victory. There weren't even any points to tally. Quick as lightning, too—that was the main thing. To see the eight uniformed guards drag the competition offstage, you'd have thought they were hauling an elephant. They called an ambulance to the circus.

There in the middle of the arena stood Berl Arbitailo, blinded by the spotlights, deafened by the orchestra and the roar of the audience, and blushing like a maiden as he readjusted the tight *bortsovka* in his groin.

The management was in a state of shock. While the circus rumbled and groaned they had a conference. Finally the ring-master appeared, white as a sheet, and managed to calm down the hall. He announced that another fighter would be put up against Arbitailo.

Who met with the same fate in the very same five seconds.

There was no describing what was going on.

To make a long story short, that evening the circus put up all its heavyweights in a row against Berl Arbitailo, and he laid out each and every one. Even got a taste for it, too, and established himself as the uncontested "World Champion of Graeco-Roman Wrestling."

The next day we all made a successful breakthrough into the circus, but Berl Arbitailo was gone. No more appearances from him. The circus wrestlers, contenders in the world championship, had all flatly refused to go on the mat with him, at any price. Wrestling was taken off the program altogether and replaced by a "Musical Eccentricity." Out went the bull and in came a turkey. We spat and hissed the whole evening through. And I never saw Berl Arbitailo on the mat again.

He became the most popular man in town. Every time he'd go down the street on his dray horse all movement would stop. People would look at him like they'd never seen him before. He was instantly made team leader of the *balagulas* in the Bureau of Horse Cartage. At all the great rallies in town they'd choose him for the presidium, and he'd sit there on three chairs at once, blushing.

Just about that time in the Soviet Union they were gearing up for the first elections to the Supreme Soviet, and our authorities, who weren't to be trifled with, advanced Berl Arbitailo as the candidate for deputy from the bloc of Communists and non-Party members. With the likes of him it was a sure bet. He had the right background. To quote the agitators in their pre-election speeches, he was born of a poor family and an honest toiler reared by the power of the Soviets, who loved his homeland like a bride and watched o'er her like a tender mother. Just like they say in the song.

I didn't see Berl Arbitailo on the mat, but I was present at his appearance before the voters at the pre-election rally, and I'll never see the likes of it again.

They held the meeting in the open at the stables of the Bureau of Horse Cartage. The candidate's office, so to speak.

The large cobbled yard was full of horse turds they hadn't managed to sweep up; the crowd was packed in so tight an apple would have had no place to fall. Instead of a rostrum they used a horse-drawn cargo platform on wheels, stacked with almost forty bags of flour. Across the bags they'd stretched a placard reading "Long Live Stalin's Constitution, the Most Democratic in the World!" From up there, the candidate for deputy, Brigadier *Balagula* Berl Arbitailo, was about to give a speech.

He climbed up the ladder to the top in a new, made-to-order suit, soiling the knees as he went. The stains made him look even more democratic and closer to the people. A good thing, too, since that tie he was wearing was running the risk of putting them off. In fact, it bothered him so much he kept shaking his head like a horse swarmed with gadflies. He'd worn the damned thing in every portrait poster they had of him all over town and here at the stables.

People's candidate, World Graeco-Roman Wrestling Champion Berl Arbitailo gave no speech. First, because it was too noisy. Even before the secret balloting the people were hollering their approval. Second, because the horses were neighing so loudly you'd think they were saluting their own man in parliament, too. What it really came down to, though, was that Berl Arbitailo wasn't used to talking and didn't know where to begin, especially from so high up. That square face of his with the little button nose, that thick neck, broader even than his head, filled right up with blood. He started coughing so loud you'd have thought he was choking on a horseshoe and even that got a storm of applause. Farther than that, though, he couldn't go. As the *balagulas* say, "Whip him or trip him, he still wouldn't budge." Not on your life.

Down below, the officials were getting a bad case of the nerves. Ten gullets at once tried prompting the start of the speech for him: "Dear Comrades! . . . Dear Comrades! . . . Dear Comrades!" All Berl Arbitailo could say to the comradely help was "Yes!"

And then he jumped down. Which came as a big surprise to a lot of people sitting in the front rows, especially the authorities. They leaped back, thinking he was making a break for it.

Not a chance. People's candidate Berl Arbitailo, our man from Invalid Street, was made of sturdier stuff. He wasn't going anywhere. He got underneath the platform, loaded with no less than forty sacks of flour and a placard reading "Long Live Stalin's Constitution, the Most Democratic in the World!" straightened out his shoulders, gave a groan, and tore the whole thing right off the ground.

The flattered electors raised an uproar like our town had never heard before. Berl Arbitailo had done something for the people far more eloquent than any speech, and it found its way right into their hearts. You could tell by their reaction his victory at the polls was a hundred per cent in the bag. Even if there'd been more than one person in the election to choose from. That there wasn't was a sign of the Party's great concern for the people. It spared them the brain-crushing effort of trying to figure out who to vote for or the pain of knowing they'd been mistaken if they picked the wrong man. There was one candidate chosen and one deputy elected. That's the way we did it here in the heartland of socialism and nowhere else on earth. But even if, God forbid, we'd had elections as phony as those in the West, in the countries of capital, with hordes of candidates scrambling for the same place, Berl Arbitailo, a simple soul, a man you could really understand, who'd found the quickest route into our hearts, would have been elected deputy all the same.

To tell you the truth, though, one circumstance almost did destroy the brilliant career of our candidate, right on election eve.

For the last few days before the election Berl had stayed

off work and was spending his time loitering around Main Street with a swarm of admirers. There was a cab stand on Main Street. Back then they didn't have taxis. Passengers were carried in horse-drawn phaetons with a convertible top and a bag of hay and empty bucket in the back.

Towering like a mountain in the coachman's seat of the first cab in line was Saxon, the old cabby, with a reddish peasant's homespun jacket on his back and a blanket on his legs. Over and over again he softly sang a line in Yiddish from the musical comedy *O, Bayadera, Mir ist Kalt in die Fis* (*Oh, Bayadera, My Feet Are Cold*). They really were, too, even in the summer. Chronic rheumatism. All year round he had to wear fur shoes and cover his legs with a blanket. He was over seventy already, but still in his prime, and he'd have kept on going to a hundred, maybe, if it hadn't been for the war.

Avrom-Iche was what they called him. The "Saxon" was a nickname he'd apparently been born with. It must have hinted at his resemblance to the biblical Samson. I never heard his last name spoken. I guess nobody knew it. He had a family name written down in his passport like any normal human being, I'm sure, but on our street we took a man at his word and last names we didn't ask for. So, Saxon it was. Look, it could have been worse.

Naturally, this had to be the day Saxon got the bright idea of stopping our people's candidate, Berl Arbitailo.

"So, sir," he asks from his box, "you're the one we're picking for deputy, eh?" Berl Arbitailo was careless enough to stop and nod.

Saxon asks the next question. "The World Champion of Graeco-Roman Wrestling are you, sir?"

This "sir" business of Saxon's was beginning to bother people.

Again a bashful nod from Berl Arbitailo.

"Interesting," says Saxon, and taking the rug off his legs, he starts to get down from the phaeton, heeling it over and nearly toppling it to its side. He strides on elephant legs to the middle of the cobblestone street and, throwing his whip to the ground, extends a hearty hand to Berl.

"Let me shake the champion's hand," he says.

Berl Arbitailo agreed. With an open heart and a simple mind. And just like the circus wrestlers before him, only the other way around now, he flew up, arched through the air, and crashed down on the cobblestones on his shoulder blades right at Saxon's feet. In a made-to-order suit and tie, no less. It was a clean victory by all the rules. The bystanders were so shocked they couldn't say a word. There was the world champion plunged to the cobblestones. Saxon dusted off his palms and wiped them on his homespun coat.

"So who's the World Champion of Graeco-Roman Wrestling?" he asked with deep interest, looking carefully around at everyone as if he were searching for the champion in the crowd.

The ex-champion was lying on the pavement, all right, but so was the people's candidate. A fact that had serious consequences. They hauled Saxon off to the police station and held him there three days and three nights. They'd have trumped up some political charges against him, too, if it hadn't been for his age and his illiteracy. That and the fact that the candidate for deputy, Berl Arbitailo himself, interceded and threatened to withdraw if they didn't let Saxon go.

It all ended happily. They let Saxon loose and he voted for Berl Arbitailo, who won unanimously at the polls. Especially since there wasn't any competition.

Everything would have worked out just fine, in fact, if it hadn't been for two things.

First: They declared open season on "Enemies of the People" again and started wiping them out mercilessly. From our town they took all the Party-promoted people, anyone who stuck his nose out just a little farther than the rest. Of all the deserving people on the street, only two got off easy. My uncle Simcha Kavalerchik, who was so quiet and inconspicuous they forgot about him altogether, and Ivan Zhukov, the legendary hero of the Civil War, who was a simple watchman at Handicraftsmen's Gardens going nowhere, and such a lush it would have been in bad taste to arrest him.

Berl Arbitailo, who might otherwise have lived a normal life, had the misfortune of being a deputy. He was one of the first they were sent to arrest. They tried taking him at night, the story goes, and eight secret policemen were so maimed nothing could put them together again.

Berl Arbitailo disappeared. Without a trace. The NKVD didn't catch him, that we know for sure. Because it got even with his whole family afterward; anyone with the name of Arbitailo was taken off to Siberia. None of them ever returned to town. Where Berl himself is nobody knows.

Years later I ran into an old townsman of mine who'd survived the war and what with this and that we got to talking about the World Championship of Graeco-Roman Wrestling. If you can believe what the newspapers said, he told me, an abominable snowman had just been discovered in the mountains of Tibet. This just might be Berl Arbitailo, he suggested. Maybe Berl had been hiding in Tibet all this time from the NKVD, he said, completely unaware that Stalin was already dead and that Khrushchev was rehabilitating everyone posthumously. My friend was a sensible individual who read the papers every day, and it's likely he was only joking. Very likely. Still, you know what they say: There's a grain of truth in every wisecrack.

185

And now for the second circumstance: Saxon's fate. He died in the war. Not at the Front—who'd send a seventy-year-old man to the Front anyway?—but with dignity all the same, like a man and a true citizen of Invalid Street.

When the Germans neared our town and the population fled on foot to the East, Saxon harnessed his horse to the phaeton and loaded it up with children. They say he seated about twenty of those kids one on top of the other, arms and legs sticking out from all sides. And even though his sick legs didn't make walking easy, he took the reins and went alongside. If he'd climbed aboard there wouldn't have been room left for the kids. Besides, it would have been too much for the horse to carry.

The phaeton was moving along the highway in a crowd of refugees when a German Messerschmidt flew over and started strafing the crowd. One of the bullets hit the horse. It keeled over in the shafts and dropped dead. Saxon and the kids in the phaeton were untouched, though. When the plane flew off, Saxon unhitched the dead horse and dragged it off to the side of the road where it wouldn't block traffic. Then he got in between the shafts and pulled that phaeton full of kids himself, no worse than the horse. They say he'd gone about five kilometers without a single stop when that Messerschmidt came back and opened fire. Saxon took several bullets and dropped in the shafts. And there he lay. Whether they pulled him off the road and buried him in the field I don't know. I doubt it. People wouldn't have been up to it. Besides, you'd have needed ten strong men from our street just to lift Saxon off the ground and there were none of them among the refugees. Our men were all at the Front and there they died, every last one.

It's made you a little sad, hasn't it? Well, what can you do? You can't spend your whole life laughing.

Anyway, I've got a little problem and maybe you can help me

out. Who was the real World Champion of Graeco-Roman Wrestling that year? You tell me. Officially Berl Arbitailo, that's clear and no doubt about it. But unofficially? We both know what Saxon did to *him*.

A Different Story/Legend Number Five

"With us, it's different." That's how Mama put it and she wasn't far from a great truth people somehow just don't like to deal with.

Judge for yourself. For two thousand years you tell a man there's no use for him and no place left to go. And just to make sure he doesn't think you're kidding, you beat him up, pillage his towns, spit in his face, cut his throat, and burn him at the stake. Any reasonable human being would have got the point long ago. Time to quit. "All right," you'd say, "the game's up. We'll slip right off the face of the earth since you're so hot to see us go."

But with us it's different. We stick around and drive people crazy. We're fruitful, we multiply, we even make a few jokes every once in a while, the kind that get around and put a man in a good mood while he's sharpening the knife to cut our throats.

Mama wasn't generalizing. She had something in mind. Specifically, what happened on Invalid Street, right in our yard. To our family, to be exact.

You know what people are like. Say a woman gets a death notice about her husband. So and so, it says, your husband has died a hero's death fighting off German Fascist aggressors for the freedom and independence of our Socialist Homeland and you, his widow, hereby get a pension. What could be clearer than that?

So, what do people do next? They cry, they tear their hair out, they think about their poor orphaned children, they even start missing that picture the deceased never had taken so his children and his children's children could see where they came from.

Time passes and it's all forgotten. You know what they say: Life takes care of itself. And the deceased gets remembered once a month, on the dot, when the pension comes, because it's too small and you can't live on it. And he never had the foresight to leave his descendants even a little something. Not even a picture. And the years go by and everything's forgotten, and how could it be otherwise, and what's the use of being shocked?

With us it was different. At first, it's true, it was the same: The death notice and the crying and the picture you didn't have and the pension you couldn't live on if you tried. But the upshot? Not even close. Wait a bit and I'll explain it all.

Take another example. A woman, a mother, a Jewish mother, watches her only son, an A student who couldn't say a dirty word if he tried, blow up in her face. The bomb rips him to shreds, short pants, leather sandals, no socks and all, leaving her nothing but a sailor's cap with the word "Aurora" on the ribbon that it tosses right into her hands.

Now, tell me, can a woman survive all that and come out normal? In some rare cases, sure. That's what you'll say and I agree. But if I tell you what happened to us, and after recovering from the shock you still try to argue you can come out of it sane, then I'm sorry, I don't agree. With one exception. It would take somebody from Invalid Street to live through it and not go crazy and even think it was all going according to plan. We're baked from different dough, you see, and with us it's different.

So let me add a little detail. The child that bomb blew up, who left his mother a sailor's cap with "Aurora" on the ribbon, was me. And the man mourned by his widow, who didn't leave a picture behind and hardly a pension you could live on, was my father. Who's alive and well to this day and who, not to repeat the same mistake, has his picture taken twice a year.

You think that's funny? . . . I don't either.

So, listen to the whole story, more like a legend you'll tell me than fact, and don't be surprised by a thing. You're dealing with Invalid Street now and, if you believe my mother, things here are different.

Everybody knows Hitler attacked the Soviet Union on the twenty-second of June 1941. Stalin wanted to be friends with him, this Hitler, and to prove it, agreed to cut up Poland. Hitler took the West and we, Stalin that is, took the East. But since Hitler was a Fascist, they said he'd overrun Poland, occupied it, and given the Poles the works. And since we were the most progressive people on the face of the earth, they said our troops had liberated the area and stretched a helping hand to the workers of southern Poland, our bloodbrother Belorussians and Ukranians, who'd groaned so long under the landowners' yoke. Admit it, it sounds nice. How can you lose?

I saw it all myself and, thanks to my good luck, my family had a lot of extra heartache.

On the captured, I mean liberated, territory, we had to establish Soviet order and make the people just as happy as we were. For the job they put my uncle in charge. He was married to my mother's other sister, and in her first letter from there she gave us the news that, regardless of what all the papers were saying, this former Poland was a heaven on earth and the prices in the market were so cheap you almost didn't need money. Then she invited us to come.

I'm no expert on paradise, but when we got to that ex-Polish town right by the latest German border and my mother made her first trip to the market, she was bewildered. Here was produce like we'd never seen and so cheap it was almost funny. The people we'd come to liberate from poverty and hunger were dressed like a bunch of capitalists in a Western movie. Even the kids. They dressed me right up in pretty new clothes, almost for nothing as Mama said, and it took me a long time just to get used to them. I'd never seen anything like them before.

A man gets used to anything, though, and I got used to the new clothes. Mama, though, never could get used to the low prices and the high quality of the goods. Every time she'd come back from the market with her baskets loaded she'd groan and torture my uncle, the Communist, with questions: Why and how and what was a person to think? And my uncle, the chief of state in town, wouldn't be able to explain a thing. Pretty soon he started hollering at her and telling her she was politically underdeveloped.

I respected my uncle. He was a Russian, not a Jew. The only reason he'd married my aunt was that he was a Communist and a genuine internationalist. Having a Jewish wife was the best sign of a first-class Bolshevik, and that's what my uncle, the Communist, was, through and through. Half-illiterate and full of self-confidence, he kept his dealings with people simple and didn't like to be contradicted. Ever. The second they'd see him on the street, even before he got close, the entire liberated population would start bowing. At first it made him angry. Later he learned to laugh. "Strange people. Don't they know I'm a simple man like them, can't they see there aren't any more lords and that everybody's equal?"

And there he was, living in the best house in town, requisitioned from the former owner, cruising around in the only car. Meanwhile, my aunt would be sending her many relatives back home these big packages every week, stuffed with woolen goods they'd bring us free of charge. My uncle didn't interfere and pretended that he didn't even notice. The way I saw it he was a real Communist on the one hand and a good husband and devoted relative on the other. My respect for him grew, and I decided that one day I'd be a warrior for the welfare of the working class just like him. The only things I decided to do without were living in the most luxurious house and getting yard goods for nothing. Thoughtless kid that I was, it didn't seem right. But then, like my mother, I was politically under-developed.

War brings lots of disappointments, and my first one was with him. The way he and the other ruling Communists behaved on the first day of the war turned my head upside down. To this day even, when I think about it, I can't feel at peace.

Everybody knows Hitler attacked us suddenly, even though we'd been years planning for the war. The day it all started I'd spent the morning swimming in the lake. At noon when I went home to eat I couldn't get through to the house. German forces were moving down the street. Mama leaned out the window and hollered at me over the heads of the soldiers to hurry up and come eat, my soup was getting cold. I was an obedient child, but I just couldn't make it. There was no place to cross. The columns moved along without a break.

It was like a dream. We didn't understand a thing. The war had been going on for hours. We didn't hear about it, though, till noon when the local radio station made a hookup with Moscow and Comrade Molotov himself came over the loud-speaker across the street from our house to let us in on it. I heard him through a fog as I stood there on the sidewalk, and Mama heard him as she leaned out the window, and the Germans heard him as they moved like a wall between Mama and me, even though they didn't get a word of it and bared their teeth at the speaker.

By nightfall we'd left home. We slept on the outskirts of town in a huge basement filled with frightened women and children, the families of Red Army officers and other local officials. At dawn my uncle crept into the crowded basement. In a whisper he woke up his wife and children, my mother and me. We made our way quietly past the bodies sleeping side by side and in the early morning fog saw a truck loaded with some women and children and their luggage. I recognized them: the families of my uncle's comrades, Communist officials like himself, who used to drop by on visits, drink vodka, and hoist the required toast to the health of Comrade Stalin.

"Quick, climb in," my uncle ordered in a whisper. "We're getting out of here."

"What about them?" I pointed to the basement door, where the wives and children of the Red Army officers slept on, completely unaware. "The Fascists'll shoot them."

The way he looked at me you could tell he was dealing with an idiot.

"We've only got one truck and there's too many of them," he hissed.

And slowly we pulled out. I sat on the luggage and the bundles, dangling my legs out the back and, sad beyond my years, watching the basement door drop from view. It already looked like the entrance of a communal grave to me.

I couldn't look him straight in the eyes any more. In the first place, I was ashamed to. Anyway, I couldn't if I tried. He was in the front beside the driver. The truck made its way along a country road, heading for the eastern end of the sleeping town. There was a gas station there where we could load up on fuel.

Here I lost my respect for him altogether. Early as it was, the fenced-off yard of the gas station where the pumps stood was already overflowing with Jews. Local Jews and Jews who'd escaped Hitler in western Poland the year before. They knew what to expect from the Germans and they'd crowded into the yard of the gas station in the hopes that people who'd come for fuel would pick them up and take them a little bit farther from a certain death.

While the driver filled up, old men and women, lots of them with babies in their arms, crowded in around us and they all said the same thing. "Don't abandon me." They pleaded. They cried. "At least take the babies!" The women were desperate. "At least save them!" And then they'd hold out these screaming lumps of swaddling.

My uncle, the top official in town, the Communist, whose life, he always said, belonged to the people, pulled a light machine gun out of the cabin, climbed into the back of the truck, aimed it at the crowd, and cursed them all.

The crowd pulled back and the truck started moving down the road. The really desperate ones ran after us, screaming, pleading, and swearing. For a hundred yards they kept on running and I thought I was going to lose my mind. Then the driver stepped on the gas and the distance between us began to grow. Finally, there was only one of them left, a boy hardly older than me, lame and on crutches, wearing the Army cap of a Polish confederate. He hopped on his crutches through the dust raised by the wheels of the truck, stumbled, and fell.

And we were saved.

What happened next I don't recall too well. Somewhere along the way a Red Army patrol stopped us. They requisitioned the truck and spent a long time checking over my uncle's papers, just to make sure he wasn't a deserter. Even though he wasn't I kept on hoping they'd shoot him on the spot.

They inducted all the able-bodied men into the Army, my uncle included, and bundled the rest of us onto railroad cars with low sidings. We were already speeding east, away from the Germans, when they bombed us to pieces.

My uncle came through the war without a scratch and had himself a bright career afterward, getting one high post after another. He'd have made it to Minister, too, if he'd had enough of an education. Even through the years of famine he had just about everything you could want, except for cream from the Milky Way, as they say. He drank a lot of vodka, too, raising the required toast to Stalin while Stalin lived and Khrushchev after that and then Brezhnev, until his heart sagged under the weight of all that fat and he died. They said in the papers that he'd been an exemplary Communist who'd died at his post in the struggle for the good of his people.

But let's get back to the time they bombed us to pieces. It happened at night while we were rushing under a full head of steam. The bombs exploded right beside us. I'd been sleeping on top of some bales of hay. My mother and baby sister were settled underneath, by the bales. In the flash of the explosion Mama saw me fly up and scatter to pieces. One of them, the sailor cap with the word "Aurora" on the ribbon, dropped into her hand.

The train didn't slow down a bit.

As you've already guessed, I didn't get blown to pieces. Otherwise, I wouldn't be here telling you all this. The bomb just threw me off the train and into the soft sand of the embankment. I wasn't even hurt in the fall. The train disappeared in the dark, trailing Mama's screams and there I stood, thirteen years old and all alone in short pants, leather sandals, and no socks. Later, when I made it to the nearest station, looking for my mother, they told me that our train had been bombed a second time and no one had survived. Which was easy to believe since the station itself was on fire and there were dead bodies scattered all around.

How I survived the next four years of the war is a story in itself and has nothing to do with this. It didn't happen on Invalid Street, and that's the only thing I'm dealing with right now.

When the war was over it was Invalid Street I recalled. I was already a soldier in the Red Army by then, even though I was still too young to serve. My artillery regiment was in Germany, just outside the town of New Brandenberg. The men had picked me up in the middle of the war, a hungry, filthy kid at a station on the Volga where I'd been living on alms, reciting poems I remembered from school. I never could get the hang of stealing. So, I became a "son of the regiment," a little soldier they'd often send under fire into places where grownups couldn't pass. I even got a couple of medals for it. That's the honest truth. When the war was over I still wasn't old enough to serve so I was one of the first to be demobilized and sent home.

Which raises a fair question. What home? I was all out of family. It had been wiped out. I didn't know where to head. That's when I got a yearning to go back to the town where I was born and find out what had happened to Invalid Street. Since I'd been in a different town at the start of the war, I hadn't even had a chance to say good-by to it. I remembered our house, a log cabin my grandfather Shaye had built with his own hands. Now as a grownup I realized that, if by some miracle that house had survived, I'd be the sole survivor and heir to the property. It was settled: I'd sell the house immediately, prices were very high after the war, and with my pockets full of money I'd start a new life as a young soldier with two medals on his chest, all his health, and not a care in the world.

What a vision. Like a driven man I rushed into town and found it burned down to the ground. I ran, rushing past the ruins and heaps of ashes, feeling out my way without mistake.

Almost all of Invalid Street was in cinders. Homes, fences —the works. Nothing left but the brick foundations overgrown with grass, the bits of charred log, and the lonely chimneys of the Russian stoves blackened with smoke. And you may not believe this, because I didn't trust it myself, but there was our house, in perfect shape. Complete with fence and big gates and the same street number as before the war and the same name on the door. My name. Well, not mine, my ancestors', but what difference did it make? I was the only heir left.

Later I found out they hadn't burned it down because it housed the Gestapo. At the time, though, I couldn't have cared less. I wasn't alone: that's all that mattered. The war was over and my house and I had survived. All of a sudden I was a man with a secure future. I stood by the wicket gate, things happening inside me. All kinds of emotions were boiling up, but I was a soldier and knew how to hold them in. And like a soldier I tried to get an exact fix on my position: I'd have to get a good price on the house and not sell it too cheap out of inexperience.

Personally, I didn't have much use for a house. The war had made me free as a bird. All my belongings were in my knapsack, two cans of meat, dry ration biscuits, and a change of underwear. And one thing more, a dagger with some sentimental value. I'd been wounded by it in the face in hand-to-hand combat. The owner of the blade had gone for my neck and missed, stabbing me in the jaw. I came out of it alive, which is more than I can say for him. My buddies rushed in to give a hand and bayoneted him in the back.

Anyway, that's how things stood. I came to the gate a pauper and opened it a rich man.

So, I opened the gate.

Now, I'd like to ask my listeners to calm down a bit and imagine the expression on my face. I couldn't see it myself, of course, but today, a long time after, when I try to describe it, I can't think of a better word than "petrified." It went stiff. I remember only one thing distinctly. I was strong and not what you'd call emotional, but, for a second, I didn't feel so good.

I was sure the house would be occupied. On my way to the gate I'd even had some fun imagining how I'd surprise the residents, declare my rights as owner, and in a grown man's voice, invite them to clear out with no hard feelings.

People were living there, all right. They stood right in the yard, in fact, looking a little bewildered at the young soldier with the knapsack on his back who'd just turned to stone by the gate.

You want to know who was standing there in the yard?

First of all, my mother. Her clothes were rags now, but she still looked the same. She stood there in a kerchief, bending over a trough full of soapsuds. She took one look at me, didn't see anyone she knew, and bent back over the trough.

Second, my sister. Over the years she'd grown into a tall teen-ager, and if she hadn't been standing next to Mama I wouldn't have known her. She didn't recognize me either, of course, and out of simple curiosity looked me over: more a child than a soldier, despite the uniform and the glittering medals. In those days soldiers back from the war used to wander from house to house trying to find out what had happened to their loved ones. Jews had it different from other people, though. The men at the Front stood a better chance of surviving than the families they'd left behind. That's why you'd see Jews in uniform wandering from house to house and not give it much of a thought. I was just one of them, gone stiff and stupid at their gate.

The third one standing there was my old aunt Riva. She'd never married. Childless and alone, she'd given her heart away to her countless nieces and nephews, including me. She'd pampered us, she'd defended us when our parents were angry, and every last one of us had grown up and forgotten all about her. The very same Riva who had been the most beautiful of my grandfather Shaye's children. Long, long ago, they said, before the Russo-Japanese War, a Czarist officer had even tried to kidnap and adopt her.

She was the one who recognized me.

Shading her eyes from the sun, she lifted her arm, looked at me for a long time, and quietly, as if it wasn't much of a surprise, said, "I think it looks like . . ."

And she called me by the name she'd given me when I was very small. I almost shouted, "Me! Yes, me!" But I didn't. I couldn't even get a word out, it seemed.

Mama raised her eyes from the trough, squinted, looked at me, tall, thin, in my sun-bleached sidecap and dusty shoes, straightened herself up and came toward me like a ghost, moving her feet sort of strangely, wiping the suds off her hands and arms. About twenty-five paces lay between us. She moved her feet and her face, like a mask, didn't express a thing. She just kept wiping the soap off her elbows, even though there was none left to wipe.

I didn't move. I've said it already, I don't have much to do with emotions and, anyway, people from Invalid Street aren't used to making a big production out of their insides. I'd lost my childhood in the war, it hadn't been very pleasant, it had turned me into a wolf cub ready to snarl at a second's notice, and the last time I'd cried was way before the war. I just stood there, nailed to the spot, and didn't move a single step to Mama. She kept on coming, recognizing me more and more the nearer she got, and when she was really close, she opened up her arms. I did something then that any reasonable man would call me names for, a scoundrel, a bastard, a convert, and he'd have been right. But Mama, my mama, who was born and bred on Invalid Street, understood and wasn't even hurt.

I wouldn't let her embrace me. That was too much. I didn't know how to cry, and you can imagine for yourself what was boiling up inside me. As it was I felt like a bomb about to burst. I yelled out an Army order: "As you were!" and Mama's arms fell to her sides.

Then, I stretched out my hand to her and said simply, like a man who'd left home just the day before, "Hello, Mama."

She didn't answer and walked silently beside me to the house. She didn't even shed a tear. Not one.

You'll say that's not the way it happens with people and I'll tell you it is. It is on Invalid Street. With us, it's different. Well, you'll tell me, who'd want to brag about it?

You lose a son. You see him die. Four years later, you get him back alive and well. Your home has a man again. He walks around the yard in his bare chest and rolled-up pants and he fixes the fence and chops the wood, and he's all grown up and the women of the house feel safe again behind his broad shoulders.

When everything calmed down, Mama told me that in a far-off village in Siberia some old woman had read her fortune. You've lost two men, she said, and as God is good you'll get them back again. For one she guessed right. I came back alive. The other was a clean miss. Mama had the death notice in her hands, and name me a government that'll pay a pension for nothing. Thanks anyway for guessing half right. Most fortune tellers just lie, but this one, God bless her, was a real crystal gazer.

Three weeks after my return from the dead the gate opens and in walks my father. In the same kind of uniform I'd worn and the same kind of knapsack on his back. And just as surprised as I was to see his family in the yard. Go ahead and laugh, but he'd come with the same intention of selling the house. The house Grandfather Shaye built. A home just might make it through the war, he thought, but a Jewish family, never.

What more can you say? Mama didn't go crazy. She didn't even seem surprised.

"With us, it's different," she said.

My father had been captured by the Germans. They killed all the Communists and Jews in the prison camps, and on that account he should have died twice. But, you see, he was born on Invalid Street and that says it all.

When they freed him, nobody praised him for being clever. That's not the custom in Russia. Just the other way around. Stalin figured that being captured was a disgrace, and the only thing that could wash it off was blood. Get yourself killed or wounded and then we'll see about forgiveness. To give a man a hand at one or the other, they'd take everyone who'd survived the Germans and put them in penal battalions. Then they'd drive them unarmed into the attack to draw fire away from the advancing troops.

A pretty picture, you'll say. Well, God help you if you're a Russian soldier from getting caught and surviving it. They've got your number. And in the penal battalion they'll finish up what they didn't get to in prison.

So how did my father survive? A natural question. Better listen to what he told me.

"I'll tell you, Son, pure luck. They ordered our penal battalion to break through the Yassko-Kishinev forces in Bessarabia. Before the assault they planted us right in the river Prut to force a crossing. As soon as we got the signal. Well, they postponed the attack and we sat there waiting in the water for weeks. No signal. It was hot as hell and we all got dysentery. The 'bloody runs,' in case you haven't heard. We stood a good chance of infecting the whole Army, so they took us to the field hospital. There we were, gushing blood, not out of any wounds, but from you know where. To wipe out the blot they needed blood and they got it. Fair and square. The blot was wiped. You know what they say: the right kind of blood for the right kind of crime."

Then he had a good long laugh and so did I and Mama and my sister, too. As a rule we like to laugh on Invalid Street. Even on occasions when others cry, we laugh. With us, it's different.

So, to tie it all up, I want to quote you the words of a very wise man everyone on our street used to think was a lunatic. Once upon a time he'd studied to be a cantor, but he flunked out, so he gave up on God and to spite the rest of us he'd sing at the top of his voice all up and down the streets. Kids used to laugh at him and grownups would shake their heads and offer him a bite to eat. A piece of bread with a little goose fat, sometimes a chicken leg. He'd sing Italian arias in Yiddish and compose the text himself. He took alms with dignity and made no secret of despising every last one of us. He was the only man on the whole street who wore a hat and tie, and whenever he gave a concert, in a yard or outside on the street, he'd first take a hammer and nail out of his pocket, bang the nail into the fence or wall, and hang his hat on it. Then he'd sing.

Anyway, once he said something I'll never forget.

"Everybody thinks Jews are so smart," he said. "Well, it's a lie. We have the most primitive minds in the world. If we had even a little bit of imagination we'd all have gone crazy long ago."

You want to know my opinion? I think he was absolutely right. And where I come from no one calls me crazy.

The Old Jerk/Legend Number Six

Years after the Second World War I came back to town again, a grownup, self-sufficient human being. I didn't recognize it any more. The town, the people—they weren't the same.

Nothing was left of Invalid Street, absolutely. Not even the name. Once there'd been massive wooden houses built by our grandfathers out of tarred logs so thick you couldn't get your arms around them; once there'd been thick log gates with forged iron bolts that seemed rooted to the ground forever; once there'd been yards swimming in gardens of every sort, scientific ones like Neyach Margolin's, wild, untended ones like our own (ah, but you should have seen the fruit in autumn!); once there'd been burdocks big as Bereleh Mats's ears growing by the fences and dill in such profusion you could see why they said our air was good for your health and people who'd been breathing it since birth grew up on the street with heroes' builds. Now, there was nothing.

Nothing but a completely different street called Friedrich Engels, packed with four-story brick houses that looked like barracks, and for gardens, a leafy twig or two sticking out of the ground—"green plantations," the newspapers called them.

The former dwellers of this once Invalid and now Friedrich Engels Street were gone, all of them. The survivors lived out their time in different parts of the town, their children scattered all over the world. Another thing was gone, too: that rapid-fire, Jewish speech, free of those damned Russian *r*'s, so full of bad grammar but so lovingly pronounced, that sweet Yiddish, *mameloshen,* spoken only by us and nowhere else on earth. You couldn't hear that any more, either.

All the old men I ran into said the same: Knock on wood, I'm the only one from the street to have made something of himself and to have brought a little pleasure to their old age by coming back to town. It couldn't have been such a bad street after all, they told me, if it produced one person at least—and such a person!

I'm a performing artist, you see, and I'd come back home to give a concert. What kind of concert? Well, my field isn't what you'd call ordinary, but they say it's got a great future. I'm a master of the artistic whistle. I whistle.* All kinds of melodies, from the classics to the contemporary songs of Soviet and even foreign composers. Some music critics are convinced the genre has great prospects for strengthening cultural ties with the countries of the West. Not to mention the fame and glory it would bring the U.S.S.R. in the world arena. The whistle knows no borders, needs no translation, and can be universally understood.

I placed third at the All-Soviet Competition of the Masters of the Artistic Whistle and earned the right to give concerts. Now I make a living with my art. If I can believe the promises of a certain reliable party, I might even go on a foreign tour soon. But maybe, as they say, I ought to wait three years first. You just have no idea how much intrigue there is in our art. I'm Jewish, you see, that's the main thing, and it complicates the picture a lot. Even when it comes to the artistic whistle.

When I got to town the old folks reminded me that my talent wasn't accidental. My grandfather on my mother's side, Shaye,

* A double entendre. In Russian, a whistler also means a liar.

205

the carpenter, had *Feiffer* ("The Whistler") for a nickname. That's what they called him, Shaika, the *Feiffer*—a positive and healthy human being. So they say, anyway. I never saw him myself; I was born years after he died. With his own mighty hands he built half the homes on our street and hundreds more on others. Even carried the logs himself, right on his back. Everything he did was first-class—the best materials, fine workmanship, and no short cuts.

Maybe that's why he produced eleven kids in all, each as much a giant as himself. Whether or not he whistled, though, as the nickname implied, I can't tell you. Even if he did, the artistic whistle didn't count for much in Czarist times and there wasn't any money in it. Maybe that's why they only had one pair of shoes in the house for all those eleven kids. In the winter they'd have to line up to go outside.

So tell me, my dear Comrade Whistler (that's what my wife and a few other people call me sometimes and they're welcome; why should I be offended? I appreciate a sense of humor)—so tell me, how is it that such a good carpenter as your grandfather, who built so many houses and was consequently always busy, couldn't buy shoes for his own children even if it was Czarist times? Aha! You think you've finally got me there, don't you? Well, hold your horses and listen to what I've got to say.

No, my grandfather didn't suffer from unemployment and yes, he worked every day of the week—except Saturdays, of course—and yes, he was a great master in his own business and they paid him accordingly. Naturally, he could have earned enough for footwear, even for eleven kids, no doubt about it.

But you're forgetting one small failing which, it turns out, even his grandchildren inherited. Or maybe I forgot to mention it. In which case I beg your pardon and now I understand your suspicious question.

This was it. My grandfather had a lot of pride. Actually, vanity, to use a term we artists have, was more like it. He was ready to see his family starve to death before he'd hurt his pride. It's no secret the best seats in a synagogue are the most expensive. That's where the richest and most respected members of the congregation sit. That's just where Grandfather sat, too. A simple carpenter, right in the very best seat in the *shul*. Everything he made went to pay for it. I don't know how religious he was, but as for pride he had more than he knew what to do with. His whole family might be swelling from hunger, but in the synagogue at least he always got respect.

That's the kind of man he was and I don't judge him for it. You know what they say, "Let the chips fall where they may, but, brother, keep your style."

My grandfather took pride in everything he did. When the First World War broke out and they wanted to call him into the Army, he didn't know which way to turn. How was he going to get out of it and not leave eleven mouths hungry, without a breadwinner? A physical deferment was clearly out of the question. With health like his they'd take him right into the Czar's private house corps. There was only one thing left to do: Ruin his health and stay by his children no matter how sick he'd be. Good, kind-hearted people gave him advice. Drink a broth made out of tobacco, they told him. So he did. With conviction and no holding back, just like everything else he ever did. And in half an hour he was dead, leaving the world eleven hungry mouths. He did get out of the draft though.

His nickname lived on in the memory of others. Shaika, the *Feiffer*. In fact it was even passed on to posterity. Not to me, though. I have a cousin, Shaye. When he was still in swaddling clothes they called him Shaika, the *Feiffer,* and he never whistled a note in his life. Meanwhile, I started whistling and even became a master. You'll tell me it's a paradox and I'll tell you there's a lot in this world that still needs exploring.

Whatever was left of Invalid Street in town, old men and women already hunched and toothless, but still broad-boned as ever, former *balagulas,* carpenters, and haulers—they all fought to get tickets to my first concert. They remembered me perfectly, it turned out. Even back then, before the war, they took me for a clever kid who'd go far. Not that they'd ever tell me to my face; you could criticize a person on Invalid Street, that was proper, but praise? Out of the question.

They applauded and made all kinds of noise, some of it appropriate and most of it not, and the management had to call them to order twice. The former citizens of Invalid Street received the entire classical portion of my repertoire with what the papers call "discreet interest." Representatives from the local authorities, who occupied all the first rows and dressed in the same semi-military suit that Stalin wore when he was alive, listened carefully and nodded their heads in time. But when I finished Chopin's A Minor Sonata and went on to a song called "Where Are You, Where Are You, Brown Eyes?" something unbelievable started to happen in the hall. Ten times they called me for an encore. I'd never had a reception like this anywhere.

" 'The Dove!' We want 'The Dove!' " cried the Jewish old men and women from the hall. They'd asked for it time and time again while I was still performing my classical repertoire, but I held out until the second part. Then, even though I hadn't been prepared to do it, I granted their wish. It was a sentimental Spanish love song beginning "When from My Native Havana I First Sailed Away . . ." Maybe the old folks connected the idea of it to me. I'd left Invalid Street, too, and sailed away, so to speak. Anyway, they asked for it like no other. So

I did it. Without rehearsal. Letting my whistle carry all my longing for the Invalid Street of old. They must have understood that out there, because they cried.

The authorities appreciated it, too. The next day the local newspaper ran a long article headlined "Our Distinguished Townsman." They only misspelled my name twice, too. There they said I'd infused my whistle in "The Dove" with the full will of the Cuban people to fight American imperialism to the end.

I didn't really appreciate how my hometown felt about me till the next day when my old mama came back home from the market. All the Jewish women there (there were still some left in town) let her pass to the front of the milk line. While they filled her can, they looked at her with respect and warmth and envy and each one came up and told her the same thing:

"Knock on wood."

I'm sorry Neyach Margolin, the *balagula*, isn't alive. I'd be interested in what he'd have to say. He usually expressed the opinion of all of Invalid Street. But there was no street now, and no opinion.

Later that evening we had a visitor from the other end of town. You'll never guess who. Rochl Elke-Chanes, the former Comrade Lifschitz, the first social activist on our street. Time had taken its toll, of course. That quiet and gentle *balagula*, Nachman Lifschitz, her husband, who used to do everything around the house while she'd be off on community business, hadn't come back from the war. She'd been taken from her duties long ago; after the war they decided Russian women could do a better job.

Despite her seventy-odd years, she was healthy as ever. Not a wrinkle on her face. And still with the sunflower seeds. Now that she had more than enough time on her hands and insomnia had crept up in her old age, she munched them day *and* night.

She sat down across from me and watched me drink tea with home preserves. Except for the grinding of her jaws she didn't make a sound. Those gray, sky-blue eyes were full of joy. To look at her, you'd have thought that my career could never have happened without a little help from her social activity. She had only one remark to make about my performance, but that said it all.

"Next to the death of Stalin," she said, "it was the greatest event in the life of our town."

She meant my success.

Before leaving town forever, I wandered its streets for a long time. How strange they seemed to me.

In the sand near a fresh construction site—it already looked like a barracks—there were some children playing. One of them, a five-year-old Jewish boy caught my eye. My heart ached to see him; it felt like my own childhood coming back to overwhelm me. The fire-red hair, the freckles, the sky-blue eyes, the strong male neck—you could see it already in the bone structure, the makings of a future powerhouse. Who else could he be but a descendant of one of the former inhabitants of Invalid Street? The next thing that happened just put the icing on the cake.

I accidentally crushed his little scoop with my foot. He got up, put his strong little hands on his hips, screwed up his face, drew a long snot with a whistle through his nose, and without the shadow of an *r*, let me have it, just like we used to do it on Invalid Street, right between the eyes.

"You old jerk!"

I knew it then; everything was far from lost.

The Author's Words in Parting

So what else did I want to tell you?

You've seen it for yourself. There isn't a Jew on Invalid Street, or anyplace else for that matter, that isn't a novel of our times. Whatever this particular branch of *Homo sapiens* has suffered and survived would have been enough for a hundred other non-Jews, with lots to spare.

Now, if a man's come through all that and still kept his head above water, you have to treat him carefully. There are strict laws in this world preserving endangered species of fauna. So why can't a humane mankind extend the law to cover Jews who've pulled through? There are just a few of them left. Implement the law and let them live. That the hand that raise the sword may wither and fall, that lips fit for insult and outrage may grow forever dumb.

The Pope's forgiven us, thank God. We're finally off the hook for crucifying Jesus Christ, another Jew. The sin now rests only on the conscience of the ancient Roman legionnaires. After two thousand years we're rehabilitated. So why won't they let us into the family of man? We're no better than others, but certainly no worse. In the brief breathing spaces along our way, between the persecutions, the pogroms, and the inquisitions, we've passed a little something mankind's way. We've given you Jesus Christ, Karl Marx, Heinrich Heine, and Albert Einstein, Arthur Rubinstein and Marc Chagall. And Invalid Street, which once made the world a nicer place to live.

211

We'll give more, too, and share it all around. But let that be, as they say, on an equal footing with the world. You to me and me to you. With open hearts and nothing up our sleeves; the way it's done between decent, self-sufficient human beings.

1971   La Moulin de la Roche, France